"Hey, hey," Ryan said softly. "It's okay."

Katie could hear his voice falter and knew his words were as much for himself as they were for her. Suddenly she knew she would do anything, would move heaven and Earth, to make him feel better...if only she knew what that anything was.

"Is there something I can do to...help?" she asked, her own voice shaking.

"You're doing it now," he answered.

"What do you mean?"

"Shh, Katie," he said. "Just let me hold you." He wrapped his arms tighter around her; it felt simultaneously natural and earth-shattering to be held by him, the man she should have given her heart to long before then. For the longest time she'd thought she was just lost without him, that she'd never be able to find someone like him again. She'd settled for Bradley, had done her best with their relationship, knowing all the time, somewhere in the very back of her mind, that he wasn't The One.

It was Ryan. It had always been Ryan.

His Pregnant Texas Sweetheart

AMY WOODS

MILLS & BOON®

First published in Great Britain 2015
by Mills & Boon, an imprint of Harlequin (UK) Limited,
Large Print edition 2015
Eton House, 18-24 Paradise Road,
Richmond, Surrey, TW9 1SR

ISBN: 978-0-263-25996-4

Harlequin (UK) Limited's policy is to use papers that are natural, renewable and recyclable products and made from wood grown in sustainable forests. The logging and manufacturing processes conform to the legal environmental regulations of the country of origin.

Printed and bound in Great Britain
by CPI Antony Rowe, Chippenham, Wiltshire

AMY WOODS

took the scenic route to becoming an author. She's been a bookkeeper, a high school English teacher and a claims specialist, but now that she makes up stories for a living, she's never giving it up. She grew up in Austin, Texas, and lives there with her wonderfully goofy, supportive husband and a spoiled rescue dog. Amy can be reached on Facebook, Twitter and her website, amywoodsbooks.com

For Babs Woods

Chapter One

Ryan Ford signaled and pulled off Main Street into the parking lot of Jenkins'. The pub's name was a testament to its no-nonsense atmosphere as a favorite local hangout. He might not be a drinking man, but he wasn't abstaining from the best hot wings in Peach Leaf, Texas. After turning off his vehicle, he headed toward the door.

Walking into that pub was like taking a step into the past. The thick, delicious scent of fry-ing chicken hit his nostrils, and the twang of country music from an ancient jukebox spilled out over heel-marred hardwood floors.

He swore not a single thing had changed, not even the barstools, which were made from salvaged tree stumps after a field nearby had caught fire a good twenty years ago. Each of the stools was carved into something unique—from horse behinds to totem poles. He couldn't help himself. The stupid old things still made him chuckle. The only thing notably absent from the setting was a thick cloud of cigarette smoke.

Ryan smiled to himself, thinking of the ruckus it must have caused with the locals when whomever had been in charge decided to do away with smoking in bars.

The wall was still decorated with photographs of famous folks who had managed to stumble into Peach Leaf on their way to somewhere else. In snapshot after snapshot, famous arms were draped over and over again around the pub's heavyset owner, Maude Jenkins, and her rail-thin husband, Jimmy. The couple smiled in each and every one, including the shot of Ryan and the rest of the senior varsity football team. A few of the photos were newer—ones Ryan hadn't seen before—and the evidence that two of his favorite people were still happy after all this time made his heart dance a little two-step.

"Well, I'll be damned." The deep, smoky voice jolted Ryan out of his thoughts and he turned from the wall, smack into the arms of Maude. "Where in the hell have you been, boy? What's it been? Fifty, seventy-five years since you've graced us with your presence?"

Ryan wrapped his arms around Maude's

broad shoulders and squeezed her into a hug. Her warm scent—a strangely comforting combination of leather and flowers—brought back memories of Friday nights after football games, when a good portion of the town had come to this same dive to celebrate wins.

"Hi, Mrs. Jenkins. How've you been?"

Maude flashed a huge, pink-lipsticked grin and held him out with her arms to give him a long once-over. "I've been fine, kid, just fine. But never mind. How the hell have you been?" She embraced him again and patted him on the back.

The woman was strong as an ox. The team had always teased her that she would make an excellent linebacker, and Maude, bless her, had never once taken offense, but rather accepted the comment as it was meant coming from clueless male teenagers—a compliment.

Those pats would have knocked the wind out of a smaller man, but Ryan held his own at six-foot-two.

"Just fine, Mrs. Jenkins. Just fine," he said, careful not to say too much.

Ryan and his father had discussed the sale of the Peach Leaf Pioneer Museum for months before they'd coordinated that morning's face-to-face meeting with the owner and director. The museum—a centerpiece of Peach Leaf and a gold mine of West Texas history—would itself become a thing of the past in the near future, as Ryan's architecture firm partnered with his dad's construction company to build a cancer treatment hospital in its place. He knew and respected Mrs. Wallace's reasons for selling her land, but the town was understandably upset about the coming change.

Arrangements were already being made for

every artifact, along with the buildings, to be preserved. The university in Austin would take all of the smaller pieces, while the old settlement homes, dating back to the 1800s, were to be transferred to a similar museum just outside of Dallas.

It bothered him a little to know that the old houses wouldn't be in their original location, but Mrs. Wallace had revealed that they were in desperate need of repair and preservation work. Her family had lovingly allowed visitors to trample through them for years, and the wear and tear had begun to take its toll. Ryan's father, for all his faults, had worked hard to find a highly recommended specialist to handle the work, and the buildings would be well cared for at their new locale.

It was for the best.

But the town wasn't likely to see it that way.

He knew that it was only a matter of time before word got out that the museum as they'd known it would be gone, replaced by a new, very modern cancer-treatment hospital, and it wasn't going to be pretty once word hit. The locals would see the benefit of a medical facility: plenty of much-needed new jobs, advanced health care nearby and so on...but they wouldn't be pleased that the hospital would cost a piece of their heritage.

Ryan stopped that train of thought; it shouldn't bother him. After all, Peach Leaf wasn't his home anymore, and after he designed the buildings, the rest was his father's problem. Ryan planned to be long gone by the time the news hit the fan.

Mrs. Jenkins chatted with him for a good half hour before finally releasing him from her grip to grab his arm and drag him over to the bar. She planted him on a stool and set to work, and before long the most decadent meal he'd had in ages was spread out in front of him like a king's feast. He took a bite of a home-style fry and savored it before tucking into his chicken and munching with contentment while Maude chattered away about the locals.

It was early in the evening, and his only companions were Mrs. Jenkins and a few people he didn't recognize, so if the President of the United States himself had walked in from the kitchen a moment later, it wouldn't have surprised Ryan more than who actually did.

If there was one thing worse than getting laid off from a job you loved, it was having to ask for an old job back that you, well...didn't.

It wasn't that working for the Jenkinses fresh

out of high school was bad; it just wasn't what Katie had wanted to do for the rest of her life. Maude and Jimmy were wonderful employers who'd treated her the absolute best for the two years she'd worked for them, but even they had been glad when Katie had accepted the offer at the museum—they had known it would make her happy, and told her they were glad for her each time she dropped by for a Coke in the years since.

Katie lost herself for a moment, letting reality slip away briefly as she thought about how she would care for the little one growing inside of her, alone, without her work at the Peach Leaf Pioneer Museum…work she loved so much. Each morning, as most people sat down at their desks following long commutes, read their emails and planned for days full of business meetings in over-air-conditioned conference rooms, Katie was busy donning petticoats and pinning her thick, shoulder-length hair up in late-nineteenth-century Gibson Girl fashion. She couldn't imagine ever enjoying another job as much. She loved teaching kids about her hometown's history, demonstrating how her ancestors wove clothing, constructed rope and baked bread, and showing adult visitors how to slow down, to take a step back in time and relearn the quiet pleasure of hard work and fruitful hands…

Three months ago, a couple of weeks after her excited pregnancy announcement, her now-ex-fiancé, Bradley, had informed her that he wasn't cut out to be a father, that he had no interest in building a family with her. Katie had been devastated…and livid. Sure, they hadn't discussed children beyond a few casual comments here and there, and yes, the pregnancy was unplanned, but she hadn't expected Bradley's reaction to be so extreme. He had never expressed a serious interest in fatherhood that she could recall, but neither had he ever specifically stated that he didn't want kids. They'd only been together for a year, and Katie always figured they would have time to discuss their hopes and dreams before planning a family. But birth control wasn't guaranteed to work and the baby was a surprise… to Katie, an incredible, lovely surprise.

Bradley hadn't shared her sentiment and had even made suggestions about how she should handle things that made her skin crawl. She'd made a big mistake in believing that Bradley was a better man than he'd turned out to be… but keeping their baby was not a mistake. Her sudden singleness and the pain of giving up the two-bedroom apartment she and Bradley had shared because it just didn't feel like home without him was a lot to carry on just her own shoulders. Plus that morning's news that in a few weeks, when the museum shut down, she would no longer have a salaried job with benefits for herself and her child. Despite all of that, and all of the other emotions churning around in her heart, Katie hadn't felt afraid.

Until now.

She had a supportive family who would stand by her every step of the way. Her parents were as open-armed as they'd always been, and she knew they would be an amazing source of support when the baby came, but Katie didn't want to lean too heavily on them. She wanted to be able to care for her child on her own. And her close friend June had welcomed Katie into the small but lovely cottage they'd shared ever since.

After Bradley had left, she'd pulled herself together and vowed to be the best mom she possibly could—plus some—to make up for the baby's absent father. For a short time, everything had been okay.

But that was before the job she loved, the career she'd built over the past five years, was threatened.

Just that morning, Katie's boss had informed her of the museum's sale to an unknown buyer, and its subsequent pending demise. The artifacts and a few of the antique buildings would be preserved elsewhere, but the museum itself, and all of the jobs it took to run it, would be eliminated. Evidently, the Peach Leaf Historical Society simply didn't have the budget to outbid the vast property's potential buyer, and a state-of-the-art hospital was to replace the museum.

Peach Leaf was a small town with more people than work, so of course Katie could see the benefit of so many potential jobs...but what about the town's history? Its culture? What about the joy the museum brought to the community through its annual fall and Christmas festivals and its children's learning programs and senior activities?

She shoved the thought aside, unwilling to let her mind linger and build anxiety and dread over something she couldn't control. She focused instead on the present.

Katie's favorite time of year was close at hand—the Peach Leaf Pumpkin Festival—and she and her coworkers had a packed schedule of events planned for that weekend. She couldn't wait for the upcoming hayride and campout, couldn't wait to pile a bunch of kids into the museum's old farm trailer and drive them the three-mile loop around the pioneer settlement, where five original homes still stood, for an afternoon of horseback riding and swimming, and a night under the stars.

Katie smiled to herself. She always made sure to pack supplies for s'mores. She knew the kids and the other staff would tease her because the treats weren't exactly "authentic pioneer food," but Katie didn't care. She treasured sharing the desserts with the children and seeing their eyes light up as they made sticky messes and huddled together for ghost stories around a glowing campfire. Plus, this year, it would give her an excuse to indulge in the chocolate cravings she'd been having lately.

A giddy rush rippled through her, just like it had when she was a kid. She was practically counting down the seconds.

But the rush was closely followed by a scratchy tightness that wrapped around her heart when she realized that this would probably be the town's last festival.

There were so many things to worry about. Aside from the most pressing issue—how to support the baby she couldn't wait to meet—there were a million other problems… How would she continue to afford her rent or gas for her geriatric truck? How could she ever replace the job that had given her so much joy, so much to look forward to?

The museum was Katie's past and present. She'd believed until this news that it would also be her future, as she'd planned to work her way up to director and take over from her boss one day, in time to send her kid to college.

Her mom and dad had taken Katie to the

Pumpkin Festival every year since they'd moved to Peach Leaf just after Katie's sixth birthday…right next door to Ryan Ford. The two had been best friends from the instant they met, despite Ryan's hesitation to hang out with a girl "covered in cooties." Like the rest of the town, the neighboring families had gathered at the festival every year, and those times were some of the best of Katie's life. It was why she'd been so thrilled when she'd gotten this job, and it was why she put every ounce of her heart into the museum.

Katie braced herself against the sudden memories of weekends with the best friend she'd eventually grown to see in a different light, and eventually lost to someone else…someone who saw that light first and claimed it.

She shook her head, pushing Ryan Ford from her memory.

Katie sighed. It was with a leaden heart that she had stepped back into the pub that late afternoon on her way home to see if her former employers needed any help. She wasn't alone anymore; she would soon have another person to provide for. When she'd stepped into the kitchen and Jimmy—pretending not to eye the curve of her growing belly—said she could come back anytime, even if there wasn't any work to be done, she wasn't sure if she should smile or cry.

She grabbed a fresh Jenkins' T-shirt to wear on her first shift. They'd agreed she would start the first of November, and Katie had just swung through the saloon doors to make her way back to her truck when her eyes landed on Ryan Ford, eating chicken wings at the bar as if it were the most normal thing in the world.

An icy tickle ran up Katie's spine and she stopped midstep.

"Ryan?" she called across to the bar, her voice shaky and thin. Maybe it wasn't really him. She'd had a long, terrible day, so maybe she was just imagining him sitting there like a mirage from her past, or a ghost; she couldn't be sure. Her feelings for Ryan Ford were so complicated, had wavered so much over the years that she couldn't be certain what would happen if it really did turn out to be him.

She didn't have to wonder much longer, because it only took one glance at his face—that incredible face she'd hated so hard, and loved even harder—to know that it was Ryan.

My Ryan, she thought, before instantly correcting herself.

He's never been yours.

He stared back at her, blinking as though

trying to see her clearly through a veil of fog. He didn't say anything for a moment that stretched out like eternity. Then he set down his fork and spoke her name, the sound of those two simple syllables rolling over his tongue making her knees go weak until they were about as useless to stand on as pillars of sand.

Katie grasped at the doorframe and steadied herself, and when she looked up again, he was crossing the room toward her.

He stopped about a foot away and seemed to second-guess his decision. She immediately cast her eyes down, unwilling to glance up again, but that didn't stop what she'd already seen. Ryan Ford had always been a pleasure to look at; there wasn't a woman in the world who would disagree. But the man who stood before Katie was...gorgeous.

He had Ryan's deep hazel eyes—tiger eyes, her mother had always called them—and Ryan's russet hair, wavy and unkempt and too long, as usual. And that was Ryan's mouth she'd seen, the bottom lip fuller than the top—lips Katie had kissed only once and wished for since. And there was Ryan's height, towering over her…making it darn near impossible to deny the truth.

A million different things rushed through her all at once. She wanted to punch him right in the face, and she wanted to wrap her arms around him. She wanted to scream at him and tell him to go back where he came from and she wanted him to hold her. She wanted to kick him in the shins, and she wanted to feel his mouth on hers. Katie couldn't make sense of any of it, and she was afraid of what she might do if he stood there much longer.

She didn't ask him why he'd done what he had done, why he'd never once contacted her after he'd driven out of town in that rusty old piece-of-junk truck—that stupid old thing Ryan had worked his ass off for just so he wouldn't have to use his dad's money—and never looked back. Why he'd refused to answer her that night when she'd asked him if he felt the same way she did. And…why he'd let her fall right out of his life, as though she'd never been important enough to hold on to.

The thoughts wouldn't stop swirling around in her head, and Katie felt as if she was going to be sick. Ryan was still standing there staring at her, his face an unreadable mask, when she sucked in the breath she hadn't known she'd been holding and pulled herself together. Before she had a chance to do anything stupid—before she had a chance to make her day even worse than the epic disaster it already was—Katie did what Ryan had done all those years ago.

She slipped past him and walked away.

Chapter Two

Footsteps crunched over the gravel behind her as Katie raced through the parking lot toward her truck, and she couldn't help but wonder if they belonged to Ryan.

Jeez. Is that what I wanted? For him to follow me?

Once, a long time ago, it would have been a resounding *yes*, but now…now her world was so completely backward that she wasn't sure.

Could this day get any worse?

"Katie," Ryan's voice rang out behind her.

So that *was* him following her. Her head and heart were in such a jumble that she didn't know how to react, so she just kept walking, digging through her purse for her keys so she would have them ready when she got to her truck. Maybe there was still a chance that the whole day had been just one big nightmare. There was still a chance—a slim one, she knew, but she would take it—that she could wake up from this and find herself back in her normal life, where each day was wonderfully similar to the one before it and where things made sense. She wanted to go back to that life, because having Ryan Ford show up in town after eight years...*that* did not make sense.

"Katie, stop!" Ryan called out, his voice somehow gentle and firm at the same time, the sound pouring over her like rain, tempting the dried-up place inside her heart—the place she'd given to Ryan when she'd been just a teenager.

And dammit if she didn't obey.

Katie halted and turned around, her pulse thumping, still reeling from the surprise of seeing him in the pub, of having him so close to her body, and from the strange mix of anger and sorrow that always welled up at his memory…and now his presence.

She'd imagined this moment before…had always envisioned herself coming face-to-face with her past love in such a way, only to meet him with poise and apathy. A single person shouldn't be allowed to turn another into mush just by his presence, yet that was exactly what he did to her. Years of time passing, of Katie maturing into a hardworking adult and now a parent-to-be, and still the sound of his voice made her want to fall into his arms.

She took a deep breath. Just because he made her feel that way didn't mean he had to know it.

"What in the world are you doing here, Ryan?"

There, she'd said his name. It tasted bittersweet on her tongue and felt raw coming out of her throat, but there it was. And it hadn't killed her.

He stopped walking a few feet away from her, the distance more comfortable to Katie than his nearness inside the bar. As long as he stayed over there, she would be fine. As long as she maintained their current proximity—as long as she couldn't smell the lemon-and-mint soap he still apparently used, and if she couldn't hear him breathing—she would be okay. She couldn't allow him to come any closer, even as she cursed herself for wanting nothing more.

"Katie, it's so good to—" He moved a foot in her direction, and she matched it with one step backward. "It's good to see you," Ryan said, shoving his hands into the pockets of his trousers. "I know you don't want to see me, but it's good to see you."

Katie met his eyes and immediately wished she hadn't.

She watched as his attention moved down to the roundness of her midsection. His eyes grew wide and he swallowed before his lips formed a thin, straight line.

He lingered there for a moment before he looked back up at her. There was softness in his gaze, along with a…hopefulness…that she couldn't have prepared herself for.

Eight years had done nothing to temper what she'd felt the night of Ryan's graduation. If she closed her eyes, she could still see the way his features had shifted when, after several long moments of standing silently in front of her, he'd finally understood what she'd been trying to say.

It had taken over a year for Katie to work up the courage to confront him…to force herself to face what she'd been feeling for far longer than she'd been able to admit, and muster enough bravery to share it with Ryan.

She loved him. Not as the best friend he'd been since childhood, but far more. Even at sixteen, she'd known something then that hadn't changed since: he was her true love… her person. No matter how hard she tried in the coming years, he would not be replaced.

At the time, she'd been naive enough to believe that loving him was enough to make him hers.

She found out soon enough that other things could come first…that other things could matter more. Things like the baby his girlfriend, Sarah, had been carrying—the baby Ryan had found out about only moments before Katie pulled him aside.

She would never forget the way he looked at her when he told her why he had to go and "do the right thing" by Sarah. Even as he'd told her that it was what he wanted, Katie could see the truth in his eyes.

For a second, a single second, she'd seen what she'd known all along. He loved her the same way—the way she wanted him to. He left that night without another word, the expression in his sad, determined eyes seared into her brain…but she knew. She wished she didn't—perhaps his leaving would have hurt less—but she knew.

When Ryan drove away that night, Sarah by his side in the cab of his old truck, along with the couple's few possessions and a jar full of cash Ryan had been saving for college, a piece of Katie went along with him.

She had cried and holed up in her room for two days, wrapped in Ryan's favorite old sweatshirt with *Peach Leaf Panthers* emblazoned across the front, but when the last tear had fallen, Katie let it drop, and she'd made a vow to let him go. Ryan was a wonderful childhood best friend and an amazing person, but she wasn't going to let his memory take away the life ahead of her. He'd taken a piece of her heart with him, but he couldn't have the rest of her, and she would make her own happiness in the world.

Even if the men she loved kept leaving her.

Katie pushed out the breath she'd been holding.

Yeah, she wanted more. She wanted a family. She wanted a husband to share her life with, and she wanted the baby inside of her. She wanted to re-create the joy that had filled her childhood home. But she was a patient woman, and she was willing to wait for those things as long as she needed to. In the meantime, she'd found a way to create a kind of makeshift happiness, and she'd found a way to embrace the parts of the past that she wanted to keep by working at the museum.

So how was it that, in one day, the world she'd built so carefully was falling down around her? And the last piece to hit the ground was Ryan Ford, who stood staring at her, waiting for her to say something.

"Ryan, I don't... I mean, I never expected to see you again," she choked out before clearing her throat. "I didn't think you'd ever come back here."

He nodded and his shoulders slumped, and Katie felt herself melt into the molten pools of gold and brown inside his eyes.

"I didn't know you still lived here, Katie. I didn't think I'd run into you like this. I'm sorry I freaked you out back there. That wasn't my intention."

Hearing him apologize tugged at Katie's heart. Why had she bolted from him? It wasn't like her to be so impolite, so unkind. And it wasn't as though he didn't have the right to visit his own hometown.

She didn't have to like him, and she didn't have to spend more than a few more seconds with him, but that didn't mean she had a right to be rude.

"No, it's okay. I'm the one who should apologize for brushing you off. Seeing you just…caught me by surprise, I suppose." She reached up and tugged at a strand of hair that had come loose from her hairdo.

Oh, God.

She still had her hair up in the Gibson Girl. She must look like a complete idiot.

And why did she care, anyway?

It was Ryan. Ryan Ford, who used to spend every weekend and afternoon at her house because he preferred it to the tumultuous atmosphere his parents' incessant fighting caused inside his own. Sweet Ryan, who used to call her Katydid like the bug, a nickname no one had used since, one which she secretly missed tremendously.

Ryan, whom she'd loved in a way she'd always known she could never find twice in a lifetime. Anger swelled inside her and Katie was grateful for its presence. It was much easier to handle than the myriad of other emotions she shoved aside.

Stupid Ryan Ford.

"Look, Katie, I—"

She held up a hand to stop him. "You don't have to say anything else." She dropped her arm to her side and before she had a chance to do anything to prevent it, his steps had eaten up all the distance between them and there he was…right there in front of her.

Her breath caught in her throat when he opened up his arms and wrapped them around her tightly. She couldn't have moved if she wanted to, and the worst part was…she wasn't sure she did.

When she could finally breathe again, his familiar smell washed over her and brought hundreds of memories with it…most of them happy, which startled her. His chest was firm and wide, and Katie resisted the urge to dissolve into him. She didn't want to think about what would happen if she gave in, about how hard it would be to let go.

He must have sensed her tension because he pulled back abruptly, balling his hands into fists at his sides as though he didn't quite know what to do with them. They stood staring at each other, the air between them a silent pool of chaos, filled with all the things they weren't able or willing to say.

And what *was* there to say, really? Yes, she'd had a crush on him growing up…more than a crush. But what he'd done that night—or rather *hadn't* done—had erased any chance of whatever unspoken feelings had been between them. The bottom line was, she couldn't trust Ryan. Couldn't trust him to be there for her and couldn't trust him with her heart.

"Look, Katie. You don't have to talk to me, and you don't have to stay. I understand if you want to get away from me. I just want you to know that I don't feel the same way."

She leaned back on her heels, just to get some feeling into her legs, which had gone numb along with the rest of her body when Ryan touched her. She looked at the ground and back up again, and he was still there.

"I really need to get home," she said. As soon as the words were out, regret tumbled through her and she had to face the fact that she really didn't want to go anywhere, least of all home, where she'd have nothing more to do than think about the job she'd lost and face her housemate's endless supply of cheer.

And to tell the truth, she wanted to talk to Ryan. She wanted to know what he'd been up to for the past near-decade and find out what kind of life he lived, what had happened with him and Sarah and the family they'd started.

Just simple curiosity. That was all.

Ryan's face fell, but he nodded. "That's fine. I understand. I've got to…get back to my hotel and work on a few things. Make some calls."

"You're not staying with your parents?" she asked. She'd just assumed they were the reason for his visit. Why else would he be back in town?

Darkness fell over his eyes, but he blinked it away in an instant. Katie had caught it, though, and she wanted to know what it meant.

"No," he said, his tone strange. "No, I'm not.

I don't...see much of them anymore...at least not my dad. Not since I left."

They weren't the only ones you left.

"Okay, well—"

"It was nice to see you, Katie. It really was. I hope it's not the last time."

She tried to keep her face neutral, but was pretty sure a funny look escaped. It was an odd thing for him to say, but then the past half hour had been odd; her whole day had been odd. This was just another slice of crazy to add to the pie.

She gave him a small grin and held up her palm in a wave before heading to her truck. Somehow she managed to unlock the door and get inside, but it wasn't until she reached to put her seat belt on that she realized her hands were shaking. She leaned forward until her head rested against the steering wheel, where she stayed until her whole body ceased its trembling and she could breathe again.

She put her key in the ignition and turned it, but the result she got was definitely not the one she expected.

Katie tried again, but all that came out of the engine was a sputtering cough.

"All right, old man. Don't do this to me. Not today."

She gave it another go and heard the same thing; the engine turned over, but it wouldn't start.

"Okay, *please*?" she begged, trying a different tactic. Maybe if she talked a little sweeter to it, the old hunk of metal would do as she asked, which really wasn't a whole lot, considering its job description.

She gave a loud groan and slammed her fists against the dashboard, throwing a fit like the smaller children sometimes did at the museum. She was about to try one more time when a sound interrupted her—a soft knock on her windshield.

Ryan.

Great.

Now she could add being a *damsel in distress* to her list of experiences. October 15 was turning out to be a very bad day indeed. If this kept up, it wouldn't hold the position of her favorite month much longer.

He motioned for her to roll down her window. That little maneuver hadn't been possible for a year or so, so she opened the door instead.

"Need some help?" he asked.

"Maybe...possibly. I don't know." She threw her hands up in the air.

Why did he look...pleased?

He gave her an utterly charming smile and she wanted to hit him.

"Jump out. Let me have a look," he instructed, and once again, she obeyed. She would really have to stop doing that… He didn't deserve it.

Once she'd hopped down, Ryan reached inside the truck and found the lever that opened the hood. He walked over and propped it open, bending to peer inside. She really wished he hadn't done that, because her eyes immediately latched on to his backside, which was even better than she remembered—a fact she would never, ever tell him.

After only a few minutes of poking around, Ryan pulled his head out from under the hood and faced her. A few streaks of grease tattooed his hands, which did nothing to make him look worse. "Your piston rings are worn," he said, looking a little too smug for his own good. "We've got to get you some new ones."

Katie ran a hand through her still-pinned-up hair, which had probably started to resemble a toilet brush by then. "How long will that take?" she asked, glancing down at her watch. Even though she wasn't going to be working at the museum much longer, Katie still had a job to do. She was determined to make this Pumpkin Festival the best the town had ever seen—even if it was the last. Especially if it was the last. And she had some shopping to do the next day and...*oh, jeez*...what if something happened, what if there was more wrong with her truck than Ryan had already discovered? She needed it to pull the trailer for the hayride Friday night.

"Well, that depends, Katydid."

She pretended to ignore the old nickname that made her pulse kick up its pace.

"On what?"

"On whether or not they have the right kind of rings at that piddly old shop on Main."

She glared at him.

Peach Leaf had always been too small for Ryan Ford.

He'd always wanted more—a fact Katie resented for the obvious implication that Peach Leaf was a small town full of small people. Including her.

He had always wanted to find something bigger…ever since they were kids. And she had always known he would. Even if Sarah's unplanned pregnancy hadn't separated him and Katie, something else eventually would have.

She would do well to remind herself of that

the next time he bent over to check her truck's engine.

"All right, well. Let me make a call and see if they have what I need." She reached inside the truck for her purse. "Maybe if they do, they can send someone over here with it."

"Nonsense," Ryan said.

"Huh?"

He rolled his eyes. "That's not necessary. You're obviously—" he raised a hand to gesture in the general area of her stomach "—in no condition to wait out here for someone from the shop. October or not, it's too hot for you to sit around outside. I'll take you over there. If they have the parts, we can pick them up and bring them back here. You have tools, don't you?"

She glanced up at him and nodded. He was serious. He really planned to take her to the store. "I don't know what you're here for or what your schedule is, but I really doubt it includes taking me over to Main Street to buy truck parts."

Ryan's jaw tightened. "You always did have trouble accepting favors."

"And you had trouble sticking around." The ugly statement was out before she could censor it, and Katie slapped a hand over her mouth. It might be true, but that didn't mean it was okay to speak out loud. Her words were harsh and hateful, and she instantly regretted their escape.

The hurt she'd caused passed quickly behind Ryan's eyes and then it was gone, but his tone became detached, cold. "Just let me take you to the store, Katie. I'll help you fix your truck and then I'll leave you alone. How's that?"

It should have been fine. It should have been

exactly what she wanted to hear. She'd been curious about what had become of Ryan Ford many times over the years. Of course she had. She'd wanted to know about his life. What kind of job he had. Where he lived. Did he stay married to Sarah…and how was the child the two had made together? But now that she'd seen him—without a wedding ring, she noticed, and looking quite well—it should have been enough to let him go permanently. He'd obviously been fine without her all this time, hadn't he? Of course he had been, or he would have made an attempt to get in touch. So why wasn't his promise enough?

Why did she find herself searching for a reason—any reason—to get him to stay a little longer?

She shoved aside all rational thought and did something supremely stupid.

"What if they don't have it?" she asked, locking up her truck before following Ryan to his vehicle—the same Jeep he'd bought with money he'd earned himself when he'd turned sixteen. Only now it was in much better shape. He'd obviously spent a lot of time and put a lot of hard work into it. She had always loved that about Ryan. He always knew exactly what he wanted and worked at it until he got it.

Too bad he didn't want me.

He opened the passenger door for Katie and held out a hand to help her inside. The gesture made her heart do a little flip. She knew to appreciate gentlemanly gestures when she saw them, which was maddeningly rare.

"Well," he said, shutting her door. He got in the driver's seat and started up the engine. "I guess they'll have to order some, which means—" he turned to grin at her "—that you'll have to wait."

"That's just the thing, though. I need my truck for the Pumpkin Festival in two days."

Ryan's eyes lit up slightly at the mention of the event. It was so subtle that if she'd blinked, Katie would have missed it.

"I volunteered to drive in the hayride at the festival this year, and I'm picking up a kiddo who doesn't have a ride to the campground."

Something changed in his eyes when she'd said those words, and Katie wondered what she could say to get that little burst of light back. Ryan had always loved the Pumpkin Fest. What had she said that bothered him?

"It's not a problem," he said, his voice low and unnervingly tender. "If your truck's not fixed in time, I'll take you, and we can use my truck for the hayride."

Ryan dropped the words and started up his Jeep as if he hadn't just offered a favor that would save her last festival. Katie was glad he didn't look over at her then because he would have caught the traces of a smile she didn't want to let him have.

Chapter Three

"It's going to take how long to fix?" Katie asked, leaning over the front counter of the auto shop on Main. The teenager behind the long Formica worktop leaned back as Katie's face drew dangerously near his own, his eyes wide with worry. Ryan bit back laughter as the grown woman and young man went back and forth futilely over how long it would take for the order of the new parts for Katie's truck to come in.

Same old spunky Katie.

There were a few changes, of course, all of them good.

She still wore her glossy dark hair long, he noted, pleased. Her eyes were the same sparkling shade of brown, almost mahogany in the daytime, but black as night when the sun went down, and then there was her body… more womanly now, more deliciously curvy in her fitted dark jeans and pink plaid camp shirt. The whole picture delighted him.

"Look, Miss Bloom," the harried-looking kid said, holding his hands out in surrender, "I know it's not what you want to hear, but the fact is we can't fix the problem without those rings, and it ain't so easy to find spare parts for a vehicle of that—" he swallowed slowly, choosing his words with meticulous care, evidently having dealt with Katie's befuddling love of her piece-of-junk vehicle on prior occasions "—production year."

Ryan and the teenager—Billy, his name tag read—exchanged a look, neither of them certain whether or not the clerk had succeeded in appeasing the aggravated woman between them. Katie shoved a fist onto each of her hips, still slim but newly curved from pregnancy—the pregnancy that sent a confusing rush of emotions through Ryan's heart each time he noticed it anew.

"Billy Greene, are you calling my truck *old*?" Katie challenged, her cheeks flushing pink.

Billy gulped again, but this time he raised his chin and met Katie's eyes.

Good, Ryan thought. Maybe she would finally let it go and accept the terms so they could leave the shop. Ryan's stomach grumbled again, as if he needed a reminder of how hungry he was. Mrs. Jenkins had given him a meal at the pub, but with all their catching up and then running into the woman who now stood in a stare-down with the auto-parts clerk, he'd only been able to scarf down a few bites.

"Miss Bloom," Billy said again, his voice squeaking a little over the words, "I've ridden in that old—" Katie's mouth dropped open but Billy ignored her "—yes, *old*, truck many a time to the Pumpkin Festival campout, and I love that thing just like all the other kids in this town."

Katie's shoulders seemed to relax ever so slightly.

"But I'm not a darn magician, and that part is pretty hard to come by." Billy took a deep breath, bracing himself once more. "So I'm real sorry, Miss Bloom, but you're just going to have to wait."

Ryan had to hold back yet another laugh at the silly exchange and, if he hadn't imagined it, Billy even stomped his foot to add finality to his statement. Katie's wound-up features loosened a little more and she leaned forward to grab her purse from the counter, pulling out a credit card. Ryan fought the urge to stop her and pay for the part himself; Katie wasn't his to take care of. He noticed he'd had to remind himself of that fact much too often in the few hours they'd spent together that afternoon.

"Oh, all right," she said, releasing a heavy breath. Billy's shoulders slipped down a bit, but his eyes betrayed remaining caution.

Ryan didn't miss a slight tremor at the corner of Katie's mouth as Billy rang up the bill, and he noticed how tightly she gripped the card as she passed it across the counter, letting go reluctantly when Billy reached out to accept it.

Why was Katie so clearly worried about money?

She'd yet to text or call anybody to let them know she was stuck with car problems. The last he'd known, after high school she'd worked at Jimmy and Maude's pub, but surely she'd moved on since… She was possibly even engaged or, worse, married—he knew from experience that pregnancy caused otherwise wedding-band-adorned fingers to swell—so where was the guy who'd gotten her into her current situation?

Katie was a grown woman now, perfectly capable of caring for a child on her own, but the thought of her being forced to do so caused a burning sensation in Ryan's chest, which he promptly blamed on Mrs. Jenkins's chicken.

As soon as she finished paying and Billy promised to call the instant her truck was ready, Ryan placed a tentative hand on Katie's shoulder, leading her out of the shop and back to his Jeep. He'd had his share of inconveniences as a result of owning an older vehicle, but his income meant they were easily handled.

As Ryan opened the passenger door and helped a deflated Katie inside, he chastised himself for caring so damn much. He owed Katie exactly nothing, and that was precisely how much he guessed she wanted to do with him. And as he glanced over at her gently rounded middle as he slid his seat-belt buckle into place, he had to fight to swallow past a lump in his throat. As much as he tried, he couldn't help but wonder about the baby inside her.

Finding out more about the developing child would open an old wound he'd rather not revisit. So he couldn't have been more surprised at himself when he opened his big mouth a second later.

He cleared his throat and the words flooded out. "When are you due?" His voice was too loud in the previously silent cab.

For a moment Katie seemed startled, as if she'd been lost in thought when he'd spoken, but then a sweet smile stretched over her lovely plump lips, causing Ryan's throat to tighten. "Well," she said, resting a palm on her belly, "that's up to this little guy." She tossed her smile over at Ryan. "But if all goes as hoped, he'll arrive in about twenty-four weeks."

Ryan nodded, kicking himself for opening

up a conversation about the very last thing in the world he wanted to discuss. Despite the years that had passed since he'd seen his ex-wife, each time he remembered the baby he and Sarah had loved and lost together, a newly sharpened knife sliced through his heart. Losing their child before its birth had been hard enough, but Sarah's gradual withdrawal from Ryan, and her eventual decision to file for divorce, had made his life nearly unbearable for a time.

He'd rebuilt the best he could manage, but it was time to fully let go and move on. He'd long since stopped missing his marriage to Sarah, but was it even possible for him to risk loving someone again, much less consider starting a family, or was he forever doomed to fresh grief on each occasion he happened to run across a random pregnant woman? Worse,

Katie was anything but a random woman, and seeing her—his first, and perhaps only, true love...the one that got away...carrying a new life—was excruciating.

How could he have offered to chauffer her and a bunch of kids around for an entire weekend of camping? It would be like forcing a recovering alcoholic to spend a couple of days locked inside a bar.

Ryan scrubbed a hand over his face. What had he been thinking?

He recalled the emotions he'd sifted through at eighteen on his graduation night, when he'd been all set to head off to college on a coveted football scholarship and Sarah had announced her pregnancy, to the whole town's shock once the news quickly spread. The townspeople were even more dismayed when Ryan and Sarah marched down to the courthouse and married on their way out of town the very next day. He'd had his reasons. Sarah made a happy bride for a while, and he still believed he'd done the right thing—at least as he'd understood it at the time.

Couples on the verge of becoming first-time parents were supposed to feel a lot of things—joy, excitement, anticipation—but disappointment and fear shouldn't have been among them. He'd been terrified, certain he didn't have what it took to be a good father at that age, still just a hardheaded kid himself. Sarah, on the other hand, had been far less surprised about the pregnancy than he, something he'd only had a chance to explore after that night had passed and he'd made enough mistakes to last a lifetime.

Ryan pulled himself out of the past and back into the present, which wasn't any less disconcerting, as he glanced over at Katie, a move that yet again threatened to knock the breath from his lungs.

She'd only become more beautiful with time.

He'd fallen in love with the self-conscious pretty girl he met as a kid when Katie and the girls' very-much-in-love young parents moved next door to his seldom-happy home. But now she was a gorgeous, confident woman—comfortable in her own skin and feistier than ever.

He made himself engage in conversation, not wanting to seem rude. After all, he was the one who'd brought it up in the first place. "You must be excited," he forced out over the lump in his throat.

As his question settled in the air, Katie's smile changed into something different and a look of apprehension crossed her features before she could hide it from him. When she spoke, though, her voice was clear and firm. "I am. Very," she said, then stopped suddenly, as if reconsidering her next comment.

"But—" Ryan offered, knowing better. He should have just let the conversation drop if he didn't want to hear more about Katie's baby. A little tingle of admonition lit through him.

That was just it. He did want to hear about it—about *them*.

No matter what he'd done or how far he'd moved from home, sitting there with his childhood best friend was like going back in time. The years of separation were no cure for what he'd felt. He supposed a piece of him would always belong to Katie Bloom.

She tossed a sideways glance at Ryan. "No *but*," she said, pausing before she went on, as if determining how much it was wise to reveal. "It's just that…well, circumstances are not ideal." She waved a gentle hand over her abdomen. "I thought I'd have things all set and ready by the time I became a mom, and…I don't. I mean, I did—" She stared out the passenger-side window as Ryan pulled his Jeep onto Main Street, unsure of what direction to head in "—but I don't anymore."

Katie looked ahead at the road, knitting her eyebrows. "Um, Ryan, where are we going?"

"To dinner," he answered, surprised at her question. Old habits died hard; he'd just assumed it was okay to bring her along to a meal with him.

"No," she said, and he glanced over at her quickly before returning his full attention to the road. It was late evening and most of the shops were closing, their owners heading home for the night, so Main Street was fairly deserted, except for a few people bustling down the sidewalk, carrying shopping bags and food containers.

Katie laughed at him. The sound filled Ryan with memories from their shared childhood—giggling together at the cinema, over-apologizing each time their hands inadvertently brushed inside the popcorn cup, him tickling her feet when he'd gotten tired of a long homework session, just to hear the infectious melody of her laughter.

"What's so funny?" he asked, and Katie rolled her eyes.

"Where do you think you're going to get dinner at this hour?" Her eyes sparkled as she teased him.

Ryan glanced at the clock on his dash. "It's only eight."

Kate's expression told him he was being an idiot. "It's Peach Leaf, Ryan. Surely you haven't been gone so long you've forgotten the limited nightlife of a small town."

Dammit, she was right. His stomach let out a groan of protest.

"It's okay," Katie said, chuckling, "you can eat at my place." She lifted her chin to indicate the road. "Just keep going and turn left up here. June and I started sharing a little house after—" she hesitated "—after I left my old apartment. You remember June Leavy from high school."

Ryan nodded.

Katie pointed up ahead. "It's this street here. Left at the stop sign."

Ryan switched on his signal and steered his truck as instructed down a narrow street lined with peach trees on the verge of shedding their leaves. The houses were familiar and soothing, and he could name just about every family who'd occupied each one before his departure—teachers, librarians, old friends from school. Some of the yards held evidence of new ownership; tricycles and shiny swing sets spoke of young families with children.

He'd found he'd really rather go back to the hotel and grab an unsatisfying snack from the vending machine than endure the generous kindness he knew to expect from Katie and her old friend, but it would be rude to turn down the invitation. He might've moved across the country all those years ago and rarely looked back, but, as Katie pointed out, Peach Leaf was a small town, immune to the rapid changes of the rest of the world, and Ryan hadn't forgotten his Southern manners.

As he followed Katie's directions and pulled into the gravel driveway of an aging but cozy-looking small blue cottage, he reminded himself that he'd agreed to spend an entire weekend with this woman—a woman he'd once loved so hard that leaving her had nearly ripped him apart—so what difference would an hour over dinner make?

The pain of loss was nothing new to Ryan, and he would just have to steady himself until the time with her passed. Then he'd do the same as he worked on the hospital plans with his father, and sat through the dreaded town meeting to inform the residents of his hometown of the timeline for razing and replacing their beloved museum.

He would endure, as he always had, and then it was back to his normal life in Seattle, the life he'd never adore but had come to tolerate for its predictable lack of complication.

A life that didn't include the inevitable hazards of love, babies…or, especially, Katie Bloom.

"I still can't believe Ryan Ford is sitting out on our deck," June whispered like a little girl at a slumber party.

Katie just rolled her eyes. No matter the subject, June was always easily excited—it was one of the countless things she loved about her friend and housemate. The woman was a card-carrying, unapologetic romantic, and over the years she'd mused more than once about how sweet it would be if Katie's childhood best friend, possibly divorced and pining over his long-lost sweetheart, swept back into town and earned Katie's love again.

In your dreams, Katie thought.

Once, long ago, she might have indulged

June's silly fantasy, but she wasn't a little girl anymore, and Ryan himself had taught her plenty about broken hearts. June could have her daydreams, but Katie preferred to stick with reality. She owed it to her soon-to-arrive little one to keep her head out of the clouds and to make decisions based on fact, rather than those tiny shivers of memory and desire that raced up her back every time she saw his face.

June reached out to grab the empty pitcher from Katie's hands as they stepped into their shared little kitchen with its buttercup-colored walls and French-blue accents. Though Katie loved it in there, it was really June's domain. Her friend had been employed at Peach Leaf Pizza since high school and was now the manager. While June enjoyed her work, deep down she hoped to open her own bakery someday. Katie often wished her friend could have her dream job sooner, rather than having to work so long to save up enough to buy a venue. Then they would both have careers they really loved…

Katie stopped what she was doing for a second as the awful recollection of her conversation with her boss pummeled into her with fresh intensity. She would have to tell June; in fact, there were a lot of unpleasant arrangements that would soon require attention. She wasn't even certain she'd be able to continue living there in the shared home that had become her sanctuary after Bradley left.

So much for the stability she wanted desperately to give her unborn baby.

Katie pulled in a steadying breath and managed to pick her heart up from the floor before June's cheery voice cut through. "I just cannot believe it. I always told you this day would come."

"Well," Katie said, her voice sounding thinner than she'd intended, "you'd better believe it because there he is. And it's not what you think—" she aimed what she hoped was a cautionary look at June "—so don't get any ideas in that wild imagination of yours."

June ignored her and pulled a large container of lemonade out of the refrigerator. She refilled the pitcher while Katie pulled her friend's fresh cobbler from the oven, the scent of warm vanilla and peaches, purchased from local farm stands and stored up for the winter months, filling the room—the perfect end to a lovely meal of rosemary-lemon chicken and potato salad. "And you expect me to believe you don't feel anything for him anymore, after the history you two share? Time can't erase everything, Katie."

How right she was.

June studied her friend's face and Katie shrugged, setting the warm dish of cobbler on a blue ceramic trivet, focusing her attention on the deepening twilight outside the kitchen window.

Katie's heart gave a little kick at the mention of her and Ryan's past. She'd come to anticipate the feeling by now. A few long-term relationships, the most recent failed but resulting in a welcome new life, and now the threat of unemployment, had done little to ease the ache that his leaving her caused back in high school. But she'd learned to ignore its presence, like a phantom pain after the loss of a limb. Nothing she couldn't handle.

Katie pulled her gaze away from the window

and pointed to a cabinet up high. June opened it effortlessly, her six-foot frame towering over Katie, who held out her hands to accept the china dessert plates she intended to use for the first time. "That's just the thing, June bug—it's history. In the past." She glanced at the stack of plates as she set them on the counter next to the cobbler dish. "Just like Bradley."

June squeezed Katie's shoulder affectionately. "At least you're finally going to use these babies."

Katie grinned. The four-place china setting was supposed to be June's housewarming present to Katie when she and Bradley bought the house they'd been admiring together, a gift June had worked extra hours to save for. When Katie told June she was returning the lot so June could have her money back after Bradley called off their plans and had the Realtor shred the house contract, June had insisted they keep and use it. The irony that its first guest would be Ryan Ford didn't escape Katie.

"Can I just say one more thing, though, and then I'll stop talking about him? I promise."

Katie tossed a skeptical look at her housemate. "What do they say about making promises you can't keep?"

June stuck out her tongue. "All right, fine. So maybe it won't be the very last thing."

"Uh-huh," Katie said.

"It's just that…well…he's hot." Mischief shone in June's eyes as she glanced at Katie. "I noticed you left that part out when you texted to let me know you two were headed up the drive."

Despite herself, Katie burst out laughing as she slid a third spoonful of cobbler onto one of the delicate black-and-white-patterned plates she'd picked out for her life with Bradley not so long ago. "I guess I just don't think of him that way. He was my friend when we were kids. I mean, the guy used to throw water balloons at me and run up behind me to shove me into the pool when I least expected it." She set the spoon aside and wiped her hands on a dishcloth. "Not exactly the stuff of fairy tales."

June just blinked, clearly not convinced.

Katie shrugged her shoulders. "Okay, fine," she said, arranging the plates on a tray with the refreshed pitcher of lemonade. "He does look good. I'll admit that much."

"What looks good?"

Katie started abruptly at the warm, low sound of Ryan's voice coming from the kitchen archway, but caught herself in time to recover before she turned to face him. “Oh, we were just admiring June’s baking.” She pulled in a deep breath as she busied herself again with the tray. “It’s unparalleled in Texas.” She winked at June, who looked a little too pleased with herself. Catching the beginning of a grin on her friend’s lips, Katie shot June a warning look.

What? June mouthed silently, and Katie deployed the stern expression she saved for rare occasions when kids got too rambunctious at the museum.

“Yep, it’s true,” June said, holding Katie’s gaze, “this is one of my favorite recipes. I love how the peaches are so ripe and delicious. They’re just gorgeous.” She winked at Katie.

The nerve.

Evidently Katie’s laser-of-doom glare didn’t work on women over twenty-five.

Some of Ryan's earlier discomfort at joining the two women for dinner seemed to have dissipated and, apparently oblivious to the ulterior meaning of the conversation going on about him, he rubbed his hands together and beamed. "Looks amazing, June," he said, turning then to Katie. "Can I take that tray from you?"

Katie regained her composure and nodded. "Of course. Thanks." She handed it over and let Ryan start out of the kitchen before she jabbed her elbow into June's side as they followed him through the open sliding-glass door and out onto the lantern-lit patio. He placed the tray onto a turquoise-painted picnic table and sat down just as June's cat, Harold, pounced onto the bench next to him, and Katie and June settled on the seat across.

"He likes you," June offered with a smile.

"He doesn't feel that way about most people, especially those of the male variety."

"What she means," Katie said as she passed out each plate, "is that he's kind of a jerk."

June pretended to look offended, though she knew as well as anyone that her own cat—the cat she and Katie adored in equal measure—was the most irritable feline who ever lived. "He's just...particular is all," June said, taking a sip of lemonade.

Katie tucked a fork into her dessert and held it up to cool. "Well, he's a terrible judge of character," she argued. "The first night I moved in, he used my suitcase as a litter box, leaving me with nothing to wear to work the next day."

June had a naughty look in her eyes. "He was just giving you a warm welcome," she soothed, and Katie nearly choked on her own laughter.

Ryan chuckled, too, and the three of them ate in silence as a welcome October breeze swept over the deck, causing the flames to dance on the citronella candles scattered about. Katie was thankful June had remembered to light them to stave off the last of the summer mosquitoes, though she had to admit the candles, combined with a couple of solar-powered iron lanterns and a string of twinkling fairy lights, gave the deck a much more romantic appearance than Katie was comfortable with at the moment.

She caught Ryan watching as she savored her last bite. He gave her an open smile that spoke of campfires and sneaking out at night to the swimming pool when they were kids, of the delicious tingle that had arisen under Katie's skin every time their limbs had brushed together.

How quickly life could change without notice, how easily the past could merge into the present…the future. Heat spread through her chest as the notion slipped into her mind, causing her to pull away from his gaze and stare down into her lap.

Ryan is the past, and only the past, she reminded herself in warning.

Letting him become anything else would only lead to sorrow again.

Katie set her shoulders back and lifted her chin. The look in his eyes as she caught them this time was both familiar and strange; it held a disconcerting mix of what they'd been and what she'd once wanted them to become. Part of her had enjoyed spending time with two of her favorite people as if not a day had passed since they were younger, but a wiser part was certain it wouldn't last.

She didn't regret inviting him to stay for dinner, and she'd been pleasantly surprised how easily his presence fit in with hers and June's. And it was kind of Ryan to offer to drive her out to the camping ground in a few days, but she knew suddenly that she couldn't ask him to stay the weekend, even though it would mean a canceled hayride and making plans for someone to drive her home. When he dropped her and the supplies off and headed back out of her life, she would feel relief.

Katie closed her eyes.

Another jolt of pain, too, but mostly relief.

Chapter Four

The next morning, Ryan stepped into the diner, half expecting all eyes to turn his way, and he was more than a little relieved when they didn't. A few friendly faces greeted him with welcome-home smiles, and Barb, the owner, remembered the booth by the window that he and Katie used to share and led him in its direction. Thankfully, his father had agreed to meet later in the day, so the restaurant wasn't teeming with regulars. Still, apprehension had settled in early that morning and didn't seem to have any plan to leave.

Though Ryan would always love his father, it would be a lie to say he liked the man already seated on the other side of his and Katie's bench.

He'd known about the cheating long before his mother found out. Ryan, only sixteen, had been the one to urge his father to tell his mother. The man's refusal, and the resulting chasm it formed between father and son, was one of the more pressing reasons Ryan had left town so young. It had taken over a year for Ryan to be able to pick up the phone to call his mom, knowing there was a fifty-fifty chance the old man would be the one to answer.

Ryan felt many things toward him now—anger, betrayal, even disgust—but not the forgiveness his father's eyes seemed to ask for as

Ryan reluctantly reached out to shake his offered hand. He wouldn't concentrate on how wrinkled it had become, or how the old man's skin seemed a little looser on his frame since the last time they'd seen each other.

"Dad," he said simply, firmly, determined not to let the sudden, unwelcome emotion creep into his words. His father didn't deserve Ryan's pity any more than he deserved to be forgiven. This was a business meeting, like the hundreds Ryan had led at his own architecture firm in Seattle, and he would treat it as such. Work was what got him through the last months of his failed marriage to Sarah, and their child's bewildering death, and it was what he dived into to forget Katie. Surely he could make it through a short meeting with George Ford.

"Son," George said, meeting Ryan's eyes with unmistakable moisture in his own.

Ryan ignored their tug on his chest, looking away to study the menu. It didn't take long to notice that it was unchanged, just like the cheery yellow walls and red-checkered tablecloths. Being there felt like stepping out of a time machine into his youth. He wished the same was true for his father; if the man looked as young and sturdy as he had years ago, it would have been a lot easier to maintain animosity. Instead, the pallor of his skin and the slight tremor of his hands made him seem almost ill, but there had been no mention of any such thing when they'd spoken on the phone. Perhaps George had a few more secrets up his sleeve.

"I'm so glad you decided to come home," he said in a wavering voice.

Ryan stopped fiddling with the menu. He would order only drinks so as not to stretch out the meeting any longer than necessary, and then he'd be on his way to tie up some loose ends before the Pumpkin Festival. The thought gave him more pleasure than it should have and Ryan's mood lifted unexpectedly. A weekend away before the serious building preparation began would be good for him; it would give him time to figure out how he planned to deal with the upcoming months of work with his father.

He gathered himself, annoyed by his father's words after being there for less than five minutes. "I've said this already, Dad—" he corrected himself "—George. I didn't *come home*. I'm here for one reason only, and after that, I'm heading back where I belong."

At least part of his statement was true.

Heading up a project of that size—a colossal, state-of-the-art cancer treatment center—was an undeniably excellent move for the company he'd built. The deal would ensure the continued prosperity of his young firm, and it would mean bigger and better future projects, all of which guaranteed he could give his employees the very best. He thought of them like family; as the owner, it was his duty to make decisions in their best interests—to care and provide for them so that they could give their own children their dreams.

Somehow it helped fill the void he felt each time he realized again that he might never have his own kids. It wasn't a solution, but it took some of the sting away.

The other reason, though, the one he'd left out, was Katie.

But his father didn't need to know that. The

old man didn't need to know anything about Ryan's life that he didn't already.

George cleared his throat and took a sip of the coffee he'd been nursing long before Ryan's arrival. "Peach Leaf is where you belong, son. This is your home."

I'm not your son anymore.

Ryan bit back the words and the surge of defensiveness they incited. "My home is in Seattle now, with my firm." He let his eyes burn into his father's as a waitress headed toward their table. "I'm here on business, as I said, and it would be a good idea to keep that in mind—" he looked up as the waitress approached "—for both of us."

He ordered black coffee and orange juice and held his tongue when George's full plate of bacon, eggs and biscuits with gravy arrived a short time later. They discussed building plans for half an hour while George ate. Ryan barely touched either of his beverages. By the time the waitress cleared their table, they'd managed to set personal matters aside and had made quite a bit of headway. Ryan grabbed the check when it arrived and held up a hand to preclude any argument.

He slipped a few bills onto the table and was halfway out of his seat when George wrapped fingers around his wrist. "Sit down, son," George said, his tone firm and authoritative. "We're not done here just yet."

Ryan silently balked but remained calm as he wrenched his hand out of his father's grip. "I beg to differ. I'm not staying to chat. I was clear when I agreed to come here that it wasn't to make amends with you—it's business only."

George closed his eyes and nodded. "Yes,

you've made yourself quite clear." He held out his hands. "But this isn't about me."

Ryan's eyes narrowed. "What are you talking about?"

George motioned to the booth's bench. "Just…have a seat, will you?"

Ryan stood motionless for a moment before he acquiesced.

"There's something we need to talk about."

He glanced at his watch, then eyed his father across the table. "I've got to go soon, but if it's important…"

George looked down into his coffee cup. "It's about Annabelle."

Ryan's ears perked up at the sound of his mother's name. They'd spoken on the phone every Thursday night since Ryan moved away, and had met annually, away from both of their homes, to vacation together, always at Ryan's expense, per his insistence. Those getaways with Mom were his favorite part of the year. He hadn't noticed any change in her at the most recent one, and he didn't recall her mentioning anything out of the ordinary. They'd had a lovely time in Athens, Greece, only a few months prior, both commenting that it would be a wonderful place to return on a future trip.

If Ryan was completely honest with himself, he'd have to admit that there was always an undertone of sadness or mild disappointment in his mom on their trips—barely detectable, but present nonetheless. She never mentioned the rift between her husband and son, and Ryan was thankful for that, but he knew she wished the two men in her life would set their differences aside and make amends. She claimed to have forgiven her husband long ago, and Ryan had no reason not to believe her; however, it didn't change his mind about the situation.

To Ryan, his father's actions were inexcusable, made worse by the fact that he'd used his son to execute the affair, while Ryan stood by—an innocent kid alongside his innocent mother, both to be made fools of when she eventually discovered the affair. The memory still brought bitterness into his heart.

The drive his father's actions had lit in him—to be a better man, a better husband, a better father—was largely why he'd insisted on marrying Sarah when she told him she was carrying their baby. But in that moment, he needed to put the past aside. This wasn't about Ryan or his father; it was about a woman they both loved dearly.

"She's sick, Ryan. Mom's had cancer for some time now."

Ryan shut his lids against his father's words as tears bit behind his eyes. He fought the threatening moisture, forcing himself to focus only on the facts before any further reaction came. It wouldn't do any good for him to get upset in the middle of a diner in a town where a single abnormal move could cause people to talk. If his mom was ill, she might not want anyone to know outside of the family, and he didn't want any speculation. Suddenly, he craved the anonymity a city like Seattle granted him.

He never should have come back to Peach Leaf. But if he hadn't...would his mother have ever mentioned her condition? He wanted to resent her stubbornness, but on some level he knew it was the very same obstinacy that coursed through his own veins.

When Ryan looked up, his father was staring at him, but with a gentle patience rather than any kind of expectation. Grateful, Ryan allowed himself to take in a mouthful of air, dizzy and aware that he hadn't been breathing properly. George's eyes were steady and Ryan realized his dad had probably known for some time, long enough to shed plenty of his own tears.

"Why are you telling me this now? And why here?" Ryan asked. As soon as he'd spoken, he regretted the words. They made him sound so selfish, when in reality his heart was on the verge of erupting, as though a grenade was trapped inside; he knew he was only using them to deflect attention elsewhere while he silently exploded.

But George didn't seem to notice, or, if he did, he kept his judgment to himself. "I would have told you sooner, son, but every time you called, you made it clear you only wanted to speak to your mother. I tried to respect that, even though I didn't much like it. And I'm sorry to tell you here, but it's the first I've seen you. I didn't want to do this over the phone."

He was right, of course, but Ryan couldn't understand why his father would even need to relay the news in the first place. He raised his chin and folded his hands on the table, only to unfold them seconds later. "Why are you the one to break this news to me?" He looked down and picked up the tip he'd left…what now seemed like hours ago. "Why didn't Mom tell me herself?"

George's eyes filled with sympathy for his

son and Ryan disliked it. Once more, he'd been in the middle of a secret without a clue.

"She knew on our last trip together, didn't she?" he said softly, his voice that of a young, scared boy.

George nodded. "Yes, she knew."

"Then why the hell didn't she tell me?" Ryan's blood boiled up beneath the surface of his skin and he folded the bill in his hands into a tiny ball. "I would have taken better care of her if I'd known. I would have made her relax more." He tossed his head back and forth. "God, Dad, we hiked all over that damn city, doing all kinds of active stuff, and she didn't say a word. Not one word." Ryan threw the bill onto the table, angry with himself for not noticing his mom was sick, but his father just gave him a slow, gentle smile.

"That's just it, son. She didn't want you

worrying or treating her like some fragile flower. She wanted to enjoy the trip with you as if she were well."

Ryan's heart broke through his ribs and landed in his gut. The threat of tears returned with a vengeance; they were even harder to hold back than when the news first hit. "But she isn't well."

George nodded at the waitress who passed by. She respectfully left the two men alone to talk despite the clock on the wall indicating it was only minutes from the lunchtime rush. "Yes, that's true." He leaned closer to Ryan and set his hands on his son's. "But her life isn't over yet, kid. There are more treatments and tests to be done, and even if the results aren't good, she's not going out without a fight. The best thing we can do is help her enjoy the hell out of her time here." He leaned back, squeezing Ryan's hands before letting them go.

Ryan couldn't stop a smile as it slipped through the deep sorrow inside him, spreading stubbornly across his mouth. "That's Mom," he said, his voice unsteady.

George gave a low belly laugh. "Damn right," he said. "That's our Annabelle."

Ryan glanced at his father, who was already lost in thought. The old man looked heart-broken, despite his brave words. Ryan still wanted to be mad at him for shattering their family's world when he was just a kid. But in that moment, all he felt was sorrow, for the years George spent being unfaithful, for Ryan's own good, if misguided, intention in marrying Sarah when they'd both known it wasn't right for either of them, and for the little girl he'd never had a chance to be a dad for, but somehow missed all the same.

He needed to see his mom as soon as possible.

And he needed to see Katie.

Maybe it was nuts, and maybe Katie's mind was worlds away from what he was thinking just then, but he could hardly wait to pick her up in a few days. What would happen over the weekend they'd spend together?

His past was full of sadness, full of regret, but did that mean his future had to be, too? If Annabelle Ford could face cancer like a bullfighter, then what was stopping Ryan from facing his future with the same tenacity?

Chapter Five

"Katie, Katie. Wake up!" June's agitated voice, rather than the usual incessant buzzing of her alarm, pulled Katie out of her dreams that Saturday morning. She sat up in bed with a start, blinking and shielding her eyes from the light of a thousand suns emitting from the cell phone June held in front of her face.

"Ryan's supposed to be here in about twenty minutes, and if you don't hustle, you're going to be late. I thought you'd already gotten up and were doing something productive in here, but when I passed your door for the hundredth time and didn't hear any noise, I got worried."

June pointed at the time on the cell phone and Katie squinted at the tiny numbers before June tossed it into her lap. "Turns out your ass is still in bed."

Katie shook her head to loosen the cobwebs a little, giving her eyes time to adjust to the daylight pouring in through her bedroom window. She shoved her hair back from her forehead and pointed toward the door. "I must have forgotten to leave it cracked last night. If my alarm doesn't work, Harold usually lets me know when it's time for his breakfast." She glared at the cat who now stood near the foot of her bed, grooming himself, obviously not upset by his failure to wake her. He must have gotten his breakfast from her roommate.

June giggled. “Not today, he didn’t. I’m surprised you didn’t hear the racket he made in my room. I’ve been up for hours.” She headed to the door. “Bathroom’s free. I’ll bring coffee when you get out of the shower.”

June winked as Katie groaned and threw back her bed sheets. “Think of it as motivation.”

The thought of coffee made Katie’s mouth water and, sniffing the air, she was pretty sure she smelled bacon, but her friend was right to suggest a hot cup of joe as a reward once she was at least a little more than half-awake. She checked her phone and, sure enough, she’d forgotten to set an earlier alarm.

She didn’t have to be out to the campsite until around ten, but she wanted to get there a little early to make sure everything was set up well in advance of the kids’ arrival. She knew enough from experience that things could go awry despite even the most meticulous planning.

Katie laughed to herself as she made the bed and grabbed her worn purple bathrobe from a hook behind her door before heading down the hall to the bathroom. There was that year her boss had forgotten to call the local ranch to drop off hay for the hayride. Instead of a hayride that one year, the kids and parent chaperones had helped Katie pile pillows and blankets into the back of her truck, and everything had worked out fine. There was the one in which Katie left the house in flip-flops, having forgotten to pack any real shoes for traipsing around the outdoors, and there was always a kid or two missing toothbrushes, but it always turned out okay. She loved that about her neighbors, her community; their resilience made it possible for Peach Leaf to survive just about anything, from minor crises to major ones.

Biting her lip, she turned on the shower and adjusted the temperature, hoping once again that the town's positive attitude and supportive nature would get them through the museum's closure. Ordinarily, there wouldn't be a doubt in her mind, but the museum was one of the last pieces of their past that Peach Leaf had to hold on to. Much of its tourism revenue depended on visitors coming to experience Texas history and to take a little taste of small-town charm, something that seemed to be fleeing a little too fast in the wake of the strip malls and chain stores sweeping across the state.

It wouldn't do any good to mope, though, Katie thought, rinsing off any last traces of soap before toweling dry. She needed to focus on keeping her head up that weekend for the sake of the kids and their parents. They would look to her to determine whether or not to worry about what the loss of the museum would mean for the townsfolk.

June knocked on Katie's door just after she'd finished dressing and blow-drying her hair, and, as promised, she stood bearing a large mug of much-needed steaming coffee when Katie beckoned her in. Katie sat on the edge of her bed, closed her eyes and took a long sip—its rich flavor was so welcome she didn't even mind that it was the decaf they'd kept in the house since Katie discovered she was expecting—then thanked June.

"Don't grovel at my feet until this weekend's over and you and Ryan Ford are back together, just like I always predicted."

Katie nearly choked on the hot, delicious liquid before managing to swallow. "I'm not going to tell you again. There is no 'me and Ryan Ford.'"

June just stood planted in the doorway, looking unconvinced. "Come on, Katie," she said, crossing her arms. "Humor me a little."

After another sip, Katie said, "I'm not sure what that means, nor do I want to know, but whatever you've got in mind, the answer is no."

Her roommate looked a little too disappointed, and Katie felt an urge to comfort her. Almost like she had years ago when she'd explained to her saddened mom that Ryan Ford would never be the older woman's son-in-law...but there was nothing to say, and talking about him would only make her more nervous than she already was, a fact she resented.

Normally, she'd be so excited she'd have gotten up well before her alarm and rushed out to the campsite ahead of the sunrise, eager to set up for a weekend of fun, but this year, the butterflies in her stomach were multiplying by the hour.

If only her stupid old truck had waited a few days to have the vehicular equivalent of a heart attack. She didn't care for the thought of depending on Ryan, but with June working and her parents out of town celebrating their anniversary, and little time to arrange another ride, she had no choice but to let him help her.

June crossed from the doorway to where Katie sat, reaching out to lay a gentle hand on Katie's forearm. "Just do one thing for me," she said, her gray eyes warm and uncharacteristically serious.

"Depends on what it is," Katie answered,

expecting a lighthearted comment despite her friend's stormy gaze.

"Just…remember that Ryan is not necessarily the same guy who walked out on your friendship and skipped town when we were kids." June's forehead creased. "Just like you're not the same girl you were then."

Katie's eyes narrowed and she tilted her head, unable to hide the skepticism she felt.

"People can change, Katie. They do change."

Staring down into her coffee, she considered her friend's statement. "Right. You're preaching to the choir here. Bradley changed his mind about me overnight."

June gave her friend's arm a tender squeeze. "Ryan's not Bradley, though, and you don't know what his life's been like since he left."

"Maybe you're right," Katie said. "People keep a lot inside sometimes, and he was always like an iceberg that way—all you could see was the top, and the rest was hidden from sight."

June nodded before speaking further. "And even though he was a sweetheart at dinner the other night, it doesn't take a genius to see there's some sadness in there."

She had a point. In the several hours she'd spent in his company that day, Ryan hadn't once mentioned Sarah or the kid the two had been expecting when they moved away.

Katie swallowed, recalling the discomfort she'd seen in Ryan's face each time his attention strayed to her growing stomach, feeling suddenly ashamed that she'd spoken about her child and hadn't inquired after his. She supposed, on some level, it was self-preservation. The news of Ryan's fatherhood on his last night of high school had been so hard to accept at the time—the man she'd only recently admitted to loving had been committed to a family with someone else, someone *not* Katie—that perhaps she didn't want to feel that way again.

Was it possible he might be going through something similar now? Seeing her pregnant?

She dismissed the thought immediately; she couldn't risk hoping for such a thing. She wasn't a love-struck teenager anymore, and she had a responsibility to more than her emotions...more than the blinding physical attraction she experienced in Ryan's presence.

She touched her belly.

If Katie ever became involved with another man, he would have to prove himself a worthy father, not just a decent man interested in the companionship of a woman. He would have to learn to love her child as much as he loved its mother…a wish she knew deep down was possibly far too much to ask. And Ryan's neglect of their friendship spoke volumes; he certainly was not the man to fill those shoes.

Katie met June's eyes and gulped down the last few drops of coffee, handing the mug to her roommate. "You're probably right about that, but don't get carried away. Nothing is going to happen between me and Ryan."

June grimaced before grabbing the cup from Katie's hand and holding it up between them. "Don't think my romanticism and superior best-friend supportiveness means I'm now your maid, missy."

Katie ignored June's comments and scooted off the bed, giving her suitcase a once-over, then zipping it closed and wheeling it to the doorway. She hoped her friend would take the hint, but June piped up again.

"I'm usually right about these things. Just you wait and see."

Walking up the steps to Katie's front porch, Ryan's nerves fired off like flare guns, and the resulting flames shot from the ends of his hair all the way down to his toes.

He'd chided himself since the second he woke up that morning in the too-firm hotel bed for thinking too much about his every move. For putting so much consideration into his choice of clothing, for spending way too long arranging his hair, for regretting having not gotten it cut at the last minute before coming back to Peach Leaf and for…being so ridiculous.

Dammit, he was acting like a girl on prom night.

He'd finally banned himself from the mirror, shoving on his favorite jeans and an old plaid shirt he wore when mowing the lawn of his Seattle home, kidding himself that he didn't care what Katie thought of his appearance. He was a grown man, for God's sake, had been married for two years to a woman he'd loved—if not perfectly, then as best he could until she'd given up on working through their problems and called it quits—and had casually dated a few since, so the absurdity of his behavior since the second he laid eyes on Katie Bloom again didn't slip past him.

But when it came to whether or not he would entertain whatever it was that rushed between them, thick and intoxicating as the first breath of summer air—he was in charge. He didn't have to let it get to him, and he damn well wouldn't.

Katie might blame him for leaving town after high school without so much as a quick goodbye, and she might hold a grudge that he'd not contacted her since, but the fact was, she wasn't blameless concerning the demise of their friendship.

She'd chosen to hide her feelings from him for far too long. Yeah, it was stupid the way he'd waited for her to see, too, what he already knew, instead of telling her the second he figured out he was in love with her, but he'd been involved with Sarah at the time and needed space to figure out how to tell his then-girlfriend that he couldn't continue dating her… because he'd fallen for his childhood friend, the girl next door.

Everything happened too late for him and

Katie; their timing was so wrong, and instead of being 100 percent honest with each other, they had both given it all up for what seemed best at the time.

It's too late to go back now, he thought, stepping up to the blue cottage's flowerpot-covered porch. If anything, all he could do now was do Katie this one last favor, as a way to apologize for his part in destroying what they'd had. And maybe, if he was lucky, they could salvage a little piece of their friendship. At least enough to make things less awkward when he came to town to visit his mom, which would be a hell of a lot more often now that he'd become aware of her illness, and—he swallowed the pain that rose to the surface each time he faced the possibility—the potentially limited amount of time she had left to spend with family.

An idea forced its way into his mind as Ryan pushed the doorbell button and waited for its ring to elicit a response: maybe he would move back to town temporarily. He could run his company and approve deals and blueprints remotely, and it would be a hell of a lot easier to help out with his mom's care if he was close by, if only for a short time.

He'd taken her out the day before, and the one before that, after meeting with his father. Annabelle Ford was a true Southern belle, but she was also genuinely kindhearted, spending most of her time volunteering wherever there was need, and she was a well-known, respected member of the Peach Leaf community. So of course she would do her best to mask the cancer's effects as long as she could, especially since, as she'd explained the day before, no one outside the family knew of its presence.

Ryan straightened his shirt and knocked on the thick oak door a few times, as the small pebble of nervousness inside him began to gather weight, threatening to grow into full-blown anxiety, just as June flung open the door, sticking out a foot to prevent a ball of fur from streaking through the crack.

"He's a bit of an escape artist if we let him out front," she said, catching Harold and scooping him up, all the while still holding the door open with one foot. She deposited the grumpy feline back into the house, wiping her hands on her jeans before holding out an arm to welcome Ryan inside.

"Morning," she said, closing the door behind her. "Can I get you some coffee for the road? Decaf only, I'm afraid."

Ryan heard June's offer of the hot beverage, but only just, his eyes focusing on Katie as she stepped from the narrow hallway into her living room, pulling a small suitcase behind her. She set a bundle of blankets and a pillow on top of the bag and looked up, her incredible dark eyes latching straight on to Ryan's, her lips spreading into a welcoming smile. She wore faded jeans, the knees worn to a lighter shade than the rest of the denim, and a long-sleeved orange shirt. Its sunset shade lent a glow to her skin, the color so close to that of milky caramel that Ryan wanted to taste her to see if she would be as sweet. And her long, dark waves were pulled to one side in a braid that fell just below her collarbone, loose pieces tickling her heart-shaped face.

Ryan wasn't sure if it was residual emotion from seeing his unwell mother or left-over stress seeking release after spending so much more time than he'd like with his father, but something broke loose inside him, and he rushed forward to his old friend, folding her into his body in a hug before he had a chance to think about his actions.

Something his mother once said crossed his mind. *Sometimes the heart knows what it wants before the head catches up.* Or some such silly thing. All he knew then was that Katie's hair still smelled like the lavender shampoo she'd always used when they were younger, and her figure fit perfectly against his, and her warm skin…

She pulled away suddenly, staring up into his face, her hazelnut-colored eyes full of surprise and concern, and something slightly more intense.

"Ryan? Are you okay?"

She shoved her hands into her pockets and gave a little uneasy laugh, and he was instantly self-conscious as he looked up in time to see June scurrying into the kitchen, leaving him alone with Katie. Thankfully, she let it go and the moment passed as she studied his expression briefly before turning to grab her suitcase again.

Armor, he couldn't help thinking. *Against me.*

He deserved her reaction. It was the cost of leaving her without a word.

Despite Katie's sunny personality, her resistance to letting life damage her optimism… he'd seen it in her eyes…he'd hurt her deeply that day and she hadn't forgiven him.

She must have sensed his discomfort with the moment of open affection because she filled the room with chatter and busied herself by getting two water bottles to go. She handed one to Ryan and he took it, picking up her suitcase with his free hand while Katie grabbed her bedding, looking way too cute as she held the giant wad of fluff against her chest.

"Let's hit the road," she said, excitement and apprehension battling in her features before she wandered out to his truck.

Ryan waved at June before following Katie out the door, hoping he'd find a way to act normal again somewhere in the twenty miles between Peach Leaf and the campground.

Chapter Six

Once they had settled into Ryan's truck and pulled out of the driveway, Katie cleared her throat, hoping the action would also shove away some of her nervousness.

"Hey, Ryan?" she asked, biting her lip. She looked down at her lap, hesitant to meet his eyes. Even though she hadn't given it much thought until June pointed it out, she had in fact noticed the wariness in his features each time the subject of children came up.

"There's somebody that we need to pick up on the way," she said, looking out the passenger window, noticing the fall decorations her neighbors set up the very second a whisper of cool air arrived to chase away the heavy summer heat. She admired a trio of pumpkins, each one resting above the other on stair steps, and a pair of friendly looking scarecrows hanging out on a porch swing, their jeans and plaid shirts stuffed with straw.

When she glanced over at Ryan, she saw his jaw flinch the tiniest bit, but other than that motion, which was so small Katie might have imagined it, he didn't give any indication of what he thought about her request.

"Not a problem," he said, tossing a smile across the bench seat, causing her heart to melt like the caramel she and June would use to dip apples for their annual Halloween party in a few weeks. “Mind if I ask who?”

Katie smiled to herself. “A little girl named Shelby. She’s one of my grandma’s children’s home kiddos.”

Ryan nodded and his eyes went soft. “Just point me in the right direction.”

She let out a puff of air, grateful he wasn’t annoyed at having to do yet another favor for her. He might look slightly different—slightly sexier, if she was honest—and the tension between them might be thick enough to skate on, but every moment she spent with him, she realized more and more that he was still Ryan Ford. Still a kind man with a heart of gold, evident to everyone, especially Katie, despite the effort he exerted to guard it from the world.

She gave him directions to the small building that served as a children's home on the north side of town and he followed them without a word, probably still feeling a little awkward about that impulsive hug back at the house.

That made two of them.

When they pulled up, she saw Ryan glance at the sign out front, indicating the organization that financed the home, and his brows knit together; she couldn't see what went on behind the sunglasses he'd donned along the way.

At least the limestone structure was a little cheerier than usual, with a few fall-themed stickers peeking out from the first-floor window glass, and a red-and-gold-leaf wreath hung from the front door.

"This is it," she said, unbuckling her seat belt. Before she'd even picked up her purse from the floor, Ryan rushed out of the driver's seat and appeared outside her door, opening it and extending a hand.

"It's not that far to the ground," she said, grinning, but he didn't crack a smile. She'd always picked on him for his impeccable Southern manners when they were kids, but she secretly loved them, all the more for the fact that he never made excuses for the way he was raised—he was a gentleman down to his core, a rare breed—and she saw now that nothing would ever change that about him. She made a note to stop teasing him about it… she didn't want to be responsible for stamping out that wonderful part of his charm.

With less reluctance than she would have liked, Katie took his offered hand, the contact of their skin creating a powerful current like the air before lightning strikes. She inhaled sharply as he helped her to the ground, his eyes never leaving hers.

"Thanks," she said, looking up at him as her feet touched pavement. He nodded, still holding her hand. She thought he might let go… was inordinately pleased when he didn't. As they walked to the front door, linked by flesh, a thousand tiny sparks flickered through her body. It was with great reluctance that she broke the bond as they arrived at the top step and she reached out to ring the bell. Ryan didn't ask any questions, just stood at her side, his presence at once both calming and unnerving.

What had happened between them since their dinner together the other evening? What was that hug about earlier that morning?

A tinge of agitation interrupted her growing awareness of the mutual attraction she couldn't deny still existed. She could feel it emanating from him almost as clearly as it danced underneath her own skin. But if Ryan thought he could just be sweet to her, do her a favor, drive her crazy by holding her hand and all would be forgiven, he was dead wrong.

She didn't have time to entertain the thought because the door opened wide and there was Ava Bloom, cheeks rosy and welcoming, silver chignon slightly askew, as the smell of apple pie baking wafted out of the doorway and blended with the crisp autumn air.

"Hi, Grandma," Katie said, stepping into the older woman's open arms.

Katie's grandmother had worked as a cook at the Peach Leaf Home for Children since before her granddaughter was born, and she didn't show signs of slowing down any time soon. Most people were uncomfortable at such a place, but her grandma and the other staff put their hearts and hands into making the foster-care facility as warm as the best real home until the kids found families, or, as her grandma always put it, until parents came to find their precious gifts.

Ava waved an arm at Ryan and he quickly obeyed, taking Katie's place in her embrace. "Well, I can barely believe my eyes," she said, squeezing him to pieces. "Ryan Ford."

She looked over his shoulder and opened her eyes wide at Katie, who just rolled her own.

The two exchanged pleasantries as Katie meandered into the kitchen, disappointed that the only pies available were still in the oven. She'd skipped breakfast that morning due to running late, and the rich smell of cinnamon, warm apples and flaky crust made her crazy.

"You leave those pies alone, kiddo," her

grandmother said, her voice carrying down the hall. “They’re not ready. And, more importantly, they’re not for you.”

She laughed to herself and peeled her eyes away from the oven. “Come on, now, I’m not that bad. I wouldn’t eat the kids’ pies,” she said, unable to keep a straight face.

Ava and Ryan joined her a moment later, and Katie noticed that Ryan’s cheeks held more color than before. He looked almost comfortable for the first time since they’d run into each other at the pub.

A surge of embarrassment rushed through her. Surely they hadn’t been talking about her. Katie’s grandma was a wonderful woman, but she wasn’t known for keeping mum, and she, like Katie’s mom, had always wanted her and Ryan to be together.

“Don’t you tell me that, girl,” the older

woman said, turning to Ryan. "I've never known someone who loves apple pie as much as this one. I used to let her eat it for all three meals when she'd stay the weekend with me," she said, laughing as she threw an arm over Ryan's shoulder. "And she never once tired of the stuff. If a person could live off apple pie—" she pointed a thumb in Katie's direction "—this one would. Especially now that she's eating for two."

"All right, Grandma," Katie said. "Thanks so much for that."

Katie watched as her grandmother's expression became serious, the lines around her mouth and eyes straightening as she put aside her normal cheer. "You're here to pick up Shelby?"

"Yes," Katie said. "Remember we talked about it on the phone last week and the director gave permission for her to come on this trip?"

Worry spiked in her grandmother's concerned features, but she didn't speak.

"Don't tell me she changed her mind."

Ava's expression relaxed slightly, and she brushed a strand of tinsel-like hair away from her face. "It's not that at all, dear, don't worry," she said, but her voice didn't portray the kind of comfort Katie imagined she'd intended.

"What is it, then?"

"Well—" Katie's grandmother clasped her hands in front of her dress "—it's just that our Shelby's had a hard week." She made a fuss of heading over to the oven to check on the baking pastries and Katie could see that she was uneasy about something. Ava nodded and stepped away from the oven, laying a hand on the kitchen's long, stainless-steel counter. "Would you two like some tea?"

"No, ma'am, but thank you," Ryan said, and Katie echoed.

"All right, then. As I was saying, things have been tough for that little girl this week."

She fumbled with a pair of reading glasses that hung from a beaded string around the tissue-paper-thin skin of her neck, and Katie noticed that she looked a little tired—a word she wouldn't normally choose to describe her endlessly energetic grandmother, a woman who had immigrated from Germany to Peach Leaf with her family as a child and who believed that pride in hard work and the love of family were the only necessities to a satisfying, happy life.

"What happened, Grandma?"

Katie reached out to take Ava's soft hand,

squeezing it gently to encourage her to go on. The nature of a children's home meant that sometimes unpleasant things happened… sometimes the kids came from terrible backgrounds and required patience and space to breathe before they were able to heal enough to accept the love of a new family. Other times, they were disappointed when prospective parents came and went without taking them home.

It was one of the reasons Katie's grandmother continued working there well past retirement age; she'd raised three happy kids of her own and then determined that she had plenty of love for more. But love wasn't always enough to make up for the really hard days… for the times when a child's heart was broken once more in an already difficult young life.

Ava took a deep breath. "Another family came this week and, well, it didn't work out."

Katie looked at Ryan and saw him swallow deeply as he peered down at his shoes. She made a note to stop being selfish and ask him about his child later that day when they had a moment alone.

Something was bothering him and he deserved her attention if he was hurting. They might not be best friends anymore, but he was part of her life, whether she wanted him to be or not, and she cared for him, even if the feeling wasn't returned.

"I'm really sorry to hear that, Mrs. Bloom," Ryan said, his voice low and soothing. He seemed unsure what to do with his hands and finally stuffed them into his pockets, tossing a nervous glance at Katie. There was that look again—a sorrowful shadow, as if an old injury had flared up again.

Katie had spent time with Shelby before and truly enjoyed the sweet, shy child's company. The little girl didn't make friends easily, and when Katie came by to visit her grandmother on occasion and Shelby was around, it took time for her to warm up enough to speak. Eventually, the two had become friends, and Katie had come to realize that any couple would be lucky to take home such an introspective, intelligent little person. She would be incredibly proud if her own child turned out to be similar. But she supposed visiting families didn't always see the girl that way; possibly her quiet, sensitive nature made them nervous that they might not be up to the task of winning the girl's soft heart.

Shelby had lived at the foster home for almost a year now, and each time Katie came to visit, she was torn between wanting to see her small friend and wanting to find that she'd gone to a forever home.

"Is there anything special we can do, Grandma? To cheer her up?" Katie asked. It had taken a while to convince Shelby to go for the Pumpkin Festival weekend anyway—she was understandably wary of spending two full days surrounded by strangers, even if there would be many other girls her own age—and Katie worried that she might have changed her mind altogether in light of the hard week she'd had.

Katie's grandma took off her red-framed lenses and rubbed the little indented spots on the sides of her nose where the bridge of the glasses had rested.

"I think she'll be okay—" She hesitated.

"Actually, I hate to say it, but the day when the child isn't sad about such a thing will be the day I start to worry."

Katie nodded, wishing, not for the first time, that she could take Shelby home herself.

"Just keep her close, give her a little TLC and some extra attention, and let her know you care about her, that she has friends."

"We can do that," Ryan said with confidence, perking up for the first time since hearing the news.

Leave it to Ryan Ford to be invested in a little girl he hadn't even met yet.

The idea wasn't crazy; after all, it was exactly how she felt about her own unborn baby…and didn't all children deserve that kind of care?

Katie's grandmother smiled and a timer buzzed, interrupting the moment. The older woman began pulling pies out of the oven, and Katie and Ryan pitched in to help.

The three of them spent a few more moments catching up. Katie explained what was going on with the museum, much to her grandmother's worry, and received assurance that work could be found at the children's home if Katie wasn't able to find anything else.

Ryan was quiet as they spoke about the museum, but Katie noticed the return of his earlier uneasiness, and she wondered again what might be bothering her old friend.

"Well, there she is!"

Ava's voice broke Katie's thoughts and she turned to see a small child with wispy blonde curls, periwinkle eyes and lovely, almost translucent skin enter the kitchen, followed closely by Linda, a smiling, motherly caretaker.

"Go say hi, honey," Linda urged gently.

Shelby's face lit up when she saw Katie, her fairy-like features and shining eyes coming to life as she ran toward her older friend.

"Well, hi there, sweetheart," Katie said, wrapping her arms around the child's tiny body and breathing in the strawberry scent of shampoo as she tucked her face into Shelby's soft curls. Katie picked up the six-year-old and swung her around, causing the musical sound of laughter to fill the room before putting her back down.

"Hi, Miss Katie," Shelby said, becoming suddenly shy when she caught sight of Ryan standing in the kitchen.

"Shelby," Katie said, holding the little girl's hand, "this is my friend Ryan." She gave Shelby's little hand a soft squeeze, trying her best to communicate that Ryan was someone safe, someone she could trust. "Can you say hello?"

Ryan left Ava's side and joined them, crouching down to meet Shelby's eyes. Katie worried that the child might be overwhelmed, but instead, she surprised Katie by studying Ryan's face without a word. He didn't say anything or push at all—just sat there and let the girl examine him, a warm, comforting smile covering his handsome features.

Katie's grandmother stood behind Ryan, biting her lip as she watched the two meet. Shelby gently pulled her hand from the safety of Katie's and reached it out to Ryan, who grasped it and gave a little shake.

"Hi, Mr. Ryan," she said softly. "Are you coming with us to camp?"

Katie and Ava exchanged a look over Shelby and Ryan, both equally amazed and pleased that the two seemed to instantly take to each other.

"I sure am," he said, giving the child a wide smile that reached all the way to his eyes.

Katie's heart softened like the apples filling the pies still cooling on the kitchen counter, as she remembered the first time they'd met years ago. They had been right around the same age as Shelby was now. She'd fallen under his spell immediately, much like this little girl. Ryan had a way of making anyone around him feel at ease and more significant than anyone else in the world. She'd loved that about him from the moment she first spoke to him at the school bus stop on the sidewalk right out front of their two houses. To this day, she remembered every word that passed between them that morning, the exact colors of the striped shirt he'd worn and the pride with which he'd shown Katie his beloved superhero lunch box.

A bittersweet ache filled her heart.

There were a lot of things she'd loved about him then.

Had she ever really stopped?

Time, silence and sore hearts had kept them separated for a long time now, but suddenly Katie wished they hadn't allowed such distance, physical and otherwise, to come between them. They should have made an effort to stay in touch. She loved her friends dearly and treasured each one of them, but even she had to admit that she'd never had another bond like she once shared with Ryan.

Katie glanced at her watch, as much to remove herself from the tender scene in front of her as to check the time. The three adults had spent far more time talking than Katie had anticipated, and while she loved catching up with her grandmother, whom she hadn't seen in a few weeks due to being so busy at work and planning for the baby, she realized that they needed to get on the road in order to make it to the campground. Katie wanted everything to be set up perfectly before kids and parents started pouring in. If this was her last Pumpkin Festival, it had to be extra special.

"Speaking of which," she said, catching Ryan's eye, "we should probably get on the road."

Ryan gave Shelby another one of his gorgeous smiles before standing up again. Katie hugged her grandmother one last time, promised to visit her sooner this time and helped Linda with Shelby's bags.

"Can I sit next to Mr. Ryan?" Shelby asked, grabbing Katie's free hand.

A tiny stab of ridiculous jealousy itched inside Katie's chest at the knowledge that Shelby didn't want to sit next to her. She knew she was being silly, and she should probably get used to it if she ever planned to share her kiddo with other people. Maybe her mother was right; maybe she was going to be a bit of a mama bear when her baby arrived.

"Of course," Katie said, offering Shelby a genuine smile. It was a good sign that she was comfortable with Ryan. She usually had a little trouble with men, and Katie knew from her background that Shelby's mom had been single before she'd given the child up for adoption, so she was glad that the little girl was able to warm up to him. Katie's grandmother had asked if the girl could ride along with her granddaughter rather than in the van that would bring the rest of the kids later, knowing Shelby would be more comfortable that Katie loved spending time with the little one.

Just before Katie lifted Shelby into the truck, the girl's features twisted with concern. "I forgot something," she said, peering over Katie's shoulder toward the home. The caretaker rushed over to ask what it was that Shelby had left inside. Katie put her back onto the ground and let her speak.

"I forgot Jeff," she said. "Can we go back inside and get him?"

"Him?" Katie asked, looking into Shelby's deep blue eyes.

"Yes," she said, offering no explanation. Katie gave Linda, the caretaker, a quizzical look.

"Jeff is Shelby's pet turtle," Linda said, patting the young girl's shoulder. "He's very clean and quiet, and he doesn't need much in the way of food or water." Linda's face was filled with tenderness for her little charge. "Shelby is very attached to him," she said, lowering her voice almost to a whisper. "It would probably make her feel a little more at ease if she could bring him along on the trip."

Katie agreed with Linda. Shelby probably would feel a little better if she had the turtle with her to bring familiarity to an otherwise new situation, but she was a little bit worried about the animal's care and about how the other children might approach him. She said as much to Linda, but her concern was met with reassurance. Still, Katie hesitated.

"I know you love the little guy," Katie said, "but don't you think he may be safer here at home while you go camping?"

Shelby's face fell, and Katie knew instantly that the turtle's presence was far more important than any inconvenience he might bring. She was just about to apologize when Ryan stepped in.

"It's all right, Katie," he said, placing a hand on her shoulder. Shelby looked up at him as if he'd hung the moon. "Besides," he said, "Jeff's home is on his back, right, Shelby?"

Shelby nodded, and Katie was glad to see the worry disappear from her sweet face.

"That's right," she said. "That's why he's my best friend," she said, "because no matter how many times my home changes, Jeff's home is always the same."

Tears pricked at the back of Katie's eyes, and all she could do was nod her agreement that it was okay for Jeff to come along. Once the turtle joined them, Katie helped Shelby get settled into the center of the cab seat, between Ryan and herself, Jeff resting happily in his plastic carrier atop Shelby's lap.

As they headed out of town, tentative rays of sunshine finally peeking out of the morning clouds, Katie couldn't help the strong surge of maternal instinct—for Shelby and for the baby growing in her womb—that wove its way through her bones.

She stole a glance over at Ryan, whose eyes were once again shielded by his aviator glasses. He must have felt her staring at him because he met her eyes over Shelby's shoulder and his lips curved up at the corners in a smile that was sweet, sexy, comforting. It made her feel safe, cared for, at home…for the first time since Bradley had walked out, for the first time since she'd lost her job, for the first time in…forever.

Chapter Seven

"Are we here?" Shelby's quiet voice piped up from the center of the bench seat, pulling Katie back from staring out of the window as she'd done most of the way there, enjoying the simple pleasure of their peaceful drive through Peach Leaf, out past the Lonestar Observatory and down the highway toward the campsite.

"Yep, this is it, sweetheart," Katie said, smoothing a few of Shelby's adorably unruly curls with her fingers as they pulled onto the dirt path. Ryan looked over at her and grinned as they passed underneath the wooden arch that read Camp Peach Leaf. Seeing the words etched into the old oak board brought back memories of warm summer nights and year upon year of Pumpkin Fests.

As they pulled farther in, Katie pointed out the river for Shelby. They both delighted in the way sunlight sparkled on the water and the peaceful sound it made as it swiftly flowed by, banked by blankets of green.

The campground belonged to the museum and was founded as a way to preserve some of the land initially owned by early Peach Leaf settlers. It was available to rent for anyone who requested it, and the guest revenue had, up until that year, helped to keep it alive and well. Through the years, it had seen summers full of laughing children, plenty of autumn events when the weather became cooler and even corporate retreats for businesspeople hungry for a taste of West Texas outdoors. And there was no shortage of activities available. The campground boasted basketball and tennis courts, a swimming pool, cabins full of bunk beds, paddleboats for the river and, Katie's favorite, stables that were home to a few gentle horses.

She couldn't wait to introduce Shelby to them, to see her eyes light up when she touched their soft muzzles, and the beautiful animals leaned in close, their large brown eyes searching for hidden apples or carrots.

But that would have to wait until later. For the next couple of hours, Ryan helped Katie and the other dozen members of the museum staff unload his and a few other trucks full of supplies. The camp facility was well stocked for meals, but the staff had brought along plenty of extra goodies, and the hay arrived as they were setting up, so Katie could finally relax a little, knowing things were coming together.

Ryan wouldn't let her lift more than a couple of pounds worth of supplies, and he kept an eye on her the whole time, making her feel slightly nervous but also a little flattered.

The past few days had been confusing, and his arrival back in town had, at first, been the last straw in a week filled with unwanted, upsetting change. But with each passing moment, each time their eyes locked or he brushed against her, and when he'd held her hand back at the children's home…Katie became more and more uncertain of what she felt. The emotions surging through her head and heart were a jumbled mess, and each minute brought something new…the comfort of having her old friend back, followed by fear that he would leave again very soon…the acute pleasure of his skin against hers, followed by the void she felt in its absence.

As she helped out as much as she could safely manage with her pregnancy, she kept a close eye on Shelby, watching as the little girl wandered around, picking wildflowers and talking to her turtle, oblivious to the adults surrounding her. She was amazed and pleased by how enamored Ryan was of their little guest. On the ride over, despite the quiet, Katie had felt a sense of calm in Shelby that she was certain the girl hadn't experienced in a long time. She was so comfortable around Ryan, and Katie couldn't blame her, but she worried about what would happen at the end of the weekend when Shelby had to go back to the children's home without her new friend.

She sent up a silent prayer that Shelby would someday find a father as caring and gentle as Ryan.

When all of the supplies were unloaded and put away, ready for the weekend, Katie stopped to grab some water from a cooler they'd set up. She caught up with some of her colleagues from the museum and spent some time speaking with the campground's caretaker, making sure he was okay and would survive the museum's upcoming closure. She was glad to hear that the older gentleman, a man of about sixty who'd lived on the grounds for years and took impeccable care of the place, had a solid retirement plan and intended to buy a small home and do some traveling abroad when his job ended in a few weeks.

Thankfully, it seemed most of her fellow workers had made plans, either before or after hearing about the plans to close the museum, and she breathed a sigh of relief, glad that they'd found a way to get by without having to drastically change their lives.

She placed her water bottle under the spigot of a large red-and-yellow canteen and filled it with liquid before closing her eyes and taking a long, refreshing sip. The weather was amazing, but she'd worked up a little sweat with the exertion of the past few hours. When she opened her eyes and they readjusted to the sun, she saw Ryan approach, openly admiring the confident way he moved, his long, strong legs carrying him quickly to her side. The work looked good on him, his cheeks full of healthy color, drawing attention to those vivid golden-brown eyes and the handfuls of chestnut hair that almost reached his shoulders.

Sometimes she forgot that he wasn't a kid anymore, and each time she saw him recently, she was struck anew by how well he'd filled out and grown into his body and all of his arresting features. *He could be a model*, she thought, forgetting herself as she stared at him while he walked toward her. Not for underwear or cologne, or anything like that, but for something much more rugged, sexier—maybe camping gear or something ultra-manly.

His lips turned up in a teasing grin as he approached, and she knew he'd caught her staring. For some reason, though—maybe because she was tired or just happy to be at one of her favorite places in the whole world—it didn't even matter. She felt oddly unself-conscious, despite having been discovered ogling her old best friend.

"If I wasn't so sure of the opposite," he said, filling his own water bottle before drawing near her side, "I would think you were admiring me just a little, Katie Bloom."

She looked down at her sneakers, her confidence from only seconds before having vanished at the sultry warmth of his voice.

"But that couldn't possibly be true, now, could it?" He playfully bumped his shoulder against hers, and her skin heated where he'd made contact.

She smiled in spite of herself and looked up into his handsome face. "Ryan, I..."

Katie couldn't seem to finish her sentence. Something had been building between them since he'd hugged her that morning, or really, since he'd stepped foot back into town, back into her life. She resented the fact that she hadn't been given a choice in the matter. He hadn't given her any warning before he showed up again, just as he hadn't when he'd left. She really wanted to be angry, to give him the silent treatment or to ignore him completely and get on with her weekend and then figure out what to do with the rest of her life… but she couldn't. Instead of logic and reason, all she had to go on was the itchy yearning in her chest that started every time he looked at her or stood within a few feet of her.

It must just be the pregnancy hormones.

She couldn't handle the way he was staring at her expectantly, seeming to want her to say something, so she changed the subject.

"Shelby seems to be doing okay," she said, nodding in the direction of the little girl.

Ryan followed her line of vision and his features softened when he caught sight of Shelby. "She does, doesn't she?" he said. "I find it really hard to believe that the right parents haven't come along and snapped her up yet." He took a sip of his water. "Anybody would be lucky to have a kid like her."

"Yes, they would," Katie agreed. "She's special, though, and she deserves the perfect family. I guess they just haven't come along yet."

He nodded and drained the last of the water from his bottle. Katie sensed that it was the right time, so she took a deep breath. "You know…I'd really like to hear about your family," she said, the words so soft she wasn't sure he'd heard them.

He didn't say anything for a long moment, and Katie worried that her instinct had been wrong, that maybe he wasn't interested in talking to her about anything personal. Perhaps he really was just doing her a favor by driving her out here and didn't have any reason to want to repair their friendship. She saw a darkness pass behind his eyes, but then it washed away. "Sarah and I didn't work out in the end," he said, his voice low and dim, tinged by what sounded like dissatisfaction or regret.

Katie nodded quietly, giving Ryan space to think and speak if he wanted to. He'd always been a private person, holding difficult things close, not letting others in until he was absolutely certain they could be trusted. Katie had always carried a sense of pride that she was one of the very few people Ryan had always been able to confide in, and she'd always fiercely guarded every tidbit of himself that he offered her.

She was only mildly surprised to find that she still wanted to be someone he could trust, still wanted to matter to him in a special way.

His voice was clearer when he spoke again, but still contained emotions that Katie couldn't quite pinpoint.

"We weren't right for each other," he said, watching as Shelby sat on the ground a few yards away and set to work weaving her bundle of flowers into a string, her little turtle in his plastic house by her side.

"I guess I knew that from the beginning," he said, turning to meet Katie's eyes. "I think the whole town did, really. People certainly weren't shy about telling me not to marry her when I did."

"So why did you?" Katie asked, the question she'd carried around with her for years slipping off the edge of her tongue with alarming ease.

It was a little crazy, she thought, how simple it could be to say words that once seemed impossible to speak. Maybe that was what friendship was…being able to come together again after a long period of separation and start over where they'd left off as if only a few seconds had passed.

But the word *friendship* still had power to make her uneasy, causing her to face once again what she'd known long ago: she didn't want to be Ryan's friend. Why couldn't she just accept that he hadn't been interested in loving her differently then, and it wasn't likely his feelings had changed? Life would have been so much easier if she'd been able to do that long ago…to simply command her heart to feel the opposite to what came naturally.

Ryan set his water bottle on the ground and rubbed his hands over his face. He motioned for Katie to join him on the grass and they both sat.

"At the time, I believed with all my heart that I was doing the right thing by marrying the mother of my child."

He'd imagined doing this with Katie many times over the years they'd spent apart—telling her how it had felt to commit his life to someone he'd liked, but not truly loved, at least not the way he did Katie. He'd enjoyed Sarah's company for a while, had reveled in the attention of the popular blonde cheerleader the last few months of high school and, looking back, he knew why he'd given in to her charm, to the way she'd worshipped him, winking at him from the sidelines at football games, cornering him by the Gatorade cooler when he'd been high on the euphoria of a game well played.

He'd wanted to feel what it was like to be wanted, the way he'd wanted Katie for so long before he'd been able to admit it, even to himself. Sarah was the opposite of Katie, the best friend whose company he'd taken for granted, thinking that she would always be there, would always be a part of his life. On some level, he'd assumed they would end up together. It seemed a natural conclusion to the instant bond and happy friendship they'd shared. But the moment he'd known, the moment he'd realized he was in love with his best friend, all he had felt was…scared. Terrified that he wasn't good enough for Katie, that somehow his father's treatment of his mother might have rubbed off on Ryan, and he couldn't risk not being perfect for the girl.

So when Sarah had offered him a way out, a chance to experience something different, he'd taken her up on it, and he'd lived with the consequences of a relationship built on something much weaker than true friendship and true love.

He looked over at his beautiful old friend, the girl next door who'd stolen his heart and never truly given it back. He'd always thought that she bore so much anger toward him for leaving without saying goodbye that she would never be able to listen to his reasons, but he'd been wrong, like he had been about so many things. He'd misjudged her, he knew now, as he turned to face her. Their shoulders were almost touching, and he suddenly wanted to close the gap between them, to be nearer to her. There was something about Katie Bloom that relaxed him, made his heart beat a little slower, a little calmer, all the while still driving him crazy with need. They'd only ever kissed once, but his body remembered, would never forget the way her lips felt against his, the way the softness of her mouth communicated a hunger beyond measure.

There was no judgment in her beautiful dark eyes now, no agitated heat rising into her gorgeous, olive-colored skin, but that didn't mean what he found instead was easier to handle. Her eyes were soft and a little sad, not sparkling with desire the way they'd been then. It didn't matter. He needed to tell her about what happened with Sarah; it was time to tell Katie the truth, regardless of the pain it might cause him to admit that he'd been wrong, that he was the one who held the majority of responsibility for ending their friendship. Even if she didn't forgive him, he owed her that.

"I tried to love her, you know," he said. "I tried so hard to be a good husband to her, to give her everything my father never gave my mother. But it wasn't enough to sustain a marriage."

A blend of sorrow and possibly jealousy washed over Katie's features. Once, he would have given his right arm to have Katie envious of another woman, but now it only added to his shame at having hurt two.

"What do you mean?" she asked, turning her whole body toward him so that their knees almost touched. He had an urge to reach out and hold her hand, to feel the soft skin enveloped in his own.

"I never told you this," he said, his voice coming out bumpier than he would have liked. Katie only stared at him, waiting for him to speak further. She was that way with everyone—patient, kind, empathetic. She took everyone's cares and made them her own. It was why she was loved by so many, why he felt so blind for having not seen that he was one of them until it was too late. It was why he couldn't understand how she could be pregnant and not have someone worrying about her every move, offering to drive to the grocery store in the middle of the night to buy any crazy thing she could possibly want.

"My father cheated on my mom. I knew about it for ages and I never told her."

"Oh, Ryan," Katie soothed. She didn't offer platitudes or say anything more, but he could feel her sympathy all the same.

"She knows now, but back then I had no idea how to break the news to her. She loved my dad so much, and to this day, I don't know if she ever had any idea until he finally came clean."

Ryan looked into the distance, fixing his

eyes on the slowly moving water of the river, watching as it flowed by, gradually eroding the bottom underneath, providing a home and sustenance to so many living things. How many summers had he and Katie spent swimming in that very water? Splashing each other and laughing as they jumped into the cool stream to escape the tickle of burning sun on their shoulders.

"He used me to do it, too. The other woman was my babysitter when Mom went to her social functions or volunteered."

He was glad Katie didn't ask about the woman. She still lived in Peach Leaf and, although he hated what had happened between her and his father, it wasn't his place to tarnish her name.

Ryan closed his eyes against the sunshine,

the heat warming his lids as it rose higher in the sky.

"Ryan," Katie said, placing a long, graceful hand on his knee. He could feel the electricity of her touch through the fabric of his jeans, and it spread through his body, setting every nerve on alert in a matter of seconds.

"You were too young," she continued, her brown eyes offering comfort and absolution. "It wasn't your responsibility to tell your mother what was going on. You had no obligation to do so. It was your father who did."

"I know that, I know," he said, and he did now. "But that didn't make it any easier."

"Well, no," Katie said. "I imagine that made it much worse, wanting your mom to know what was happening, but also not wanting to hurt her."

He'd never spoken of this with anyone, had

never shared this secret that, had it escaped at the time, would have wrecked multiple lives and hurt a woman he loved so much. It felt… freeing…to share it with Katie, and he knew he could have done so long ago and she would have kept it to herself, taken it to her grave. But his parents were only part of the equation. He needed to explain why he'd chosen Sarah over Katie. Understanding what happened with his mom and dad might help her comprehend his reasons.

"Eventually, he did tell Mom," Ryan said, "and she forgave him." His hands balled into fists at the memory. He'd been so confused and angry that his mother could so easily let go of his father's betrayal. "I couldn't believe she did it so easily, but that's how Mom is."

Katie's eyes clouded over. "It's because she loves him, and it's unconditional," Katie said, squeezing his knee with her fingers. “She might have been angrier and more hurt than you ever knew…after all, you were a child then, and she wouldn’t have wanted you to carry the burden of her sadness…but she loved him anyway. She would forgive anything.”

Ryan wanted Katie’s words to mean that she had forgiven him, but it was dangerous to read into them that way. He still needed to apologize; she couldn’t let him off that easily.

“It was only one time with Sarah before we got married,” he said, his frankness causing Katie to look away. “Only one time and she swore she was on the pill. I’d never been with anybody else…she was my first…and she said the same about me. I believed her, and I truly thought it was risk-free because it was the first time for both of us,” he said abruptly.

Katie was suddenly very interested in the

grass between her sneakers. He shared her discomfort, but he had to do this anyway.

“It never once crossed my mind that she might end up pregnant.”

Katie gave him a look that said *Really?* and he almost laughed, thankful she had the ability to bring light to such a serious moment.

“Ryan, you don’t have to tell me this stuff. You don’t owe me—”

He placed his hand over the one she’d laid on his knee.

“I want to, though, Katie. Let me, please.”

She nodded, her expression so open and sweet that he gave in to the temptation to brush a strand of dark, silky hair away from her face. She pulled in a breath when he did so, and it took all the strength in him to keep from kissing her.

“So when Sarah told me she was carrying my kid, I thought of all that stuff with my parents…about the way I'd felt knowing my dad wasn't the man I'd always thought he was. And I knew I couldn't let my own son or daughter go through the same thing. Imagine if I'd let Sarah have the baby alone, and wasn't around to watch my child grow up." Ryan almost choked on the words. "Even if things weren't perfect with Sarah, I believed that we could learn to love each other eventually."

"You could have, I suppose. After all, it happens in arranged marriages all the time in other cultures, and many of them have much lower divorce rates," Katie said, offering him a grin.

And she was right. *But it never happened with Sarah.*

"I tried, and she tried, but it wasn't enough…" He wanted to tell her about their baby, but his heart was already raw from sharing so much, and he couldn't bring himself to do it just then. "After a while, we agreed to an annulment, and there were no hard feelings. I admitted it was never going to work, and Sarah admitted that she lied about being on the pill, though I'll never know if she meant to get pregnant."

A few trucks rambled up the camp's dirt road, bringing excited families, and Katie glanced at her watch.

"You were just kids, Ryan. I don't blame you for what happened with you and Sarah."

He could tell she wasn't being completely truthful, but then again, neither had he. He'd left out his child—the most painful part—a part he wasn't sure he could share yet. And he'd still left out the part about being in love with Katie back then…about the feelings he still carried around and wasn't sure would ever dissipate entirely.

Katie squeezed his knee one last time and then pulled her hand away, making a move to get up, but Ryan grabbed her hand and drew her back down to where he sat. "I'm not finished," he said, his eyes pleading with her to hear him out.

"It's okay, you don't have to—"

"Katie," he said, reaching for her other hand, holding them both when he caught it. "I'm sorry."

Her shoulders fell back and she blinked at him.

"I'm so sorry I left you. I never should have moved away without telling you goodbye." He looked at their clasped hands, turning Katie's over to stroke her palm with his thumb. "I never should have moved away at all."

As he watched her face for an indication of what she might be feeling, pools of water welled up behind her eyes, but Katie closed her lids before they fell, pulling a hand away to swipe at her face. Ryan smiled at her when she looked up at him again, and he opened his arms, inviting her in, drawing her close to his chest, memorizing the way she felt against his body so he'd have something to hold on to when she walked away to greet the weekend guests.

Chapter Eight

Katie could have waited another minute to hear if Ryan had more to say, but the second he'd touched her hand, something strange happened inside her, something that had been building since that morning when he'd wrapped her in his arms, and now he'd done it again.

Damn that Ryan Ford.

Actually, it was herself she should be cursing, for letting him slip under her skin again, for letting him remind her why she'd missed him so much.

She'd wanted his apology for so long, but now that she had it, instead of filling the hole he'd dug in her heart in his absence, all it created was a new open space. The only thing that would fix this one was Ryan himself… all of him.

When they joined the others, Katie tried to put aside thoughts of Ryan as she went through the motions greeting campers and their parents like she did every year, but this time it was on autopilot. All she could think about was how good it felt to be held by Ryan, how astoundingly different it was than the way she'd always felt in Bradley's arms.

Ryan's hugs were full of emotion, full of all the things going on in his own heart; and now that she thought about it, they always had been.

Pieces came together in her mind, creating a whole picture from previously disjointed fragments of their shared past. Ryan coming over in the middle of the night, throwing pebbles at Katie's window until she woke up and joined him in the swing on her parents' front porch, his face always unreadable as he'd hold her hand in the darkness. She never thought much of it back then, never questioned something that was so pure, so dear, as the sensation of his little-boy hand on hers when they were just children. She adored him then and was so caught up in every moment he shared with her that, she understood now, she'd been unable to see that he was hurting.

She'd heard his parents argue on occasion, but her own parents never spoke of it. Mr. and

Mrs. Ford were upstanding people, untouched by tragedy or heartache…or so she'd believed.

What Ryan had chosen to share with her that afternoon broke a little piece of her heart. It meant that even a couple she'd always admired—for their beautiful home, their gorgeous family photographs and the incredibly elaborate dinners Ryan's mother put together and invited them to sometimes—were not perfect. Their happiness—a happiness Katie would have sworn was real—was an illusion. She'd been fooled like the rest of the town by the Fords' smoke and mirrors.

And if the marriage of two such people, pillars of the community, admired by all, was tarnished…how could she and Ryan ever hope for a happy ending?

Katie almost gasped as the thought came, billowing in like a breath of wind as she helped set up the girls' cabin alongside the other moms, all of them thrilled to share a weekend with their kids.

The thought was almost deceptive in its quiet arrival, in its seeming innocence: *I want a happy ending.*

Not just that, she admitted, letting the truth sink under her skin and soak into her bloodstream…she wanted a happy ending with Ryan Ford.

She had loved Bradley, had wanted things to work out with him. He'd been kind and thoughtful and loving when they'd first met, and she had envisioned a future with him… had given him her whole heart, only to have it smashed into pieces when she'd happily shared the news of her pregnancy.

Oh, she wanted this baby so badly.

She'd been livid when Bradley had the

nerve to suggest that she shouldn't keep it. He'd never wanted kids, he'd said, had never imagined himself as a father. They had never formally discussed it, and their year together had gone by so fast—Bradley busy building his career as a policeman, and Katie working hard at the museum, all the time believing that she'd finally have a chance at getting over Ryan, at moving on to make a full life.

She'd learned the hard way that she'd been living in a dream; she'd been made a fool of. Bradley told her that his job made it illogical and irresponsible for him to be a father. What would happen if he was injured or even killed in an accident, leaving Katie and a child behind? He hadn't listened to reason when she tried to explain that plenty of the other police officers had families, and they were okay. Besides, Peach Leaf had a crime rate equivalent to that of a utopia; it was one of the safest places in Texas, and Bradley's own office had the statistics to back that up. But her attempts to talk him into making a family with her were futile, and it took her way too long to see past his flimsy excuses and understand that he'd never meant for them to have one anyway.

"Katie!"

A voice rang out behind her as she tucked the edges of her sheets into the bottom bunk of a bed near the front of the cabin. Shelby had dibs on the top bunk and Katie agreed, having been tricked into a deal of reading the little girl not one but two bedtime stories that night when she knew she'd be exhausted after riding and the hayride.

She turned to see Lucy Haynes behind her

and an ever-growing Shiloh alongside in her wheelchair.

"Oh, my gosh, hi!" she shouted, startling Shelby, who promptly hid behind her leg, gripping a handful of Katie's jeans with all her might.

Lucy rushed forward and hugged Katie. "I haven't seen you in ages," Lucy said. "How's the baby coming along?" She held Katie out at arm's length and studied her belly. "You look amazing, by the way."

"You're sweet," Katie answered, smiling at her friend. "You've been so busy with the observatory fund-raiser this year that I almost forgot what you look like."

"Same old," Lucy said, "emphasis on the *old*."

Katie laughed at her decidedly *not* old friend and reached down to hug Shiloh, who was starting to look exactly like her aunt, her red wavy hair longer and more beautiful than ever, making the two look like fairy-tale princesses.

Shiloh peeked around Katie's leg. "Who's this?" she asked, her voice friendly and inviting enough to coax out a shy Shelby.

"This is my friend Shelby," Katie said, placing a gentle hand behind the little girl's shoulder blades, urging her to step forward and say hello. She didn't have to do much more because Shelby was instantly entranced by Shiloh's hair.

"She looks just like a princess," Shelby said.

Shiloh thanked her new friend profusely and the two girls went off, Shelby promising to show Shiloh around the campground.

Katie and Lucy followed them out of the cabin, running into a few other Peach Leaf women. Katie hoped Ryan was having a good time catching up with the guys, though if she were honest, she really wanted him all to herself.

"I heard Ryan Ford's back in town," Lucy said as they walked outside into the gorgeous afternoon.

More trucks had arrived, full of excited families ready for the hayride and a day of fun. Katie had joined the rest of the museum staff for a meeting earlier to get everything organized, but the crew had done this so many years in a row that everyone knew the drill by heart. Most of the cooking and facility upkeep would be handled by the caretaker and his staff, but the regular museum employees helped out everywhere they could and made sure everyone had a good time.

Katie saw her friends Liam and Paige Campbell setting up a face-painting booth with their son, Owen, and their adorable toddler, Winnie. Owen's face was painted to look like a comic-book character and Katie saw Ryan stop to admire the art, winking at Katie as she and Lucy passed.

"Speak of the devil," Lucy said, earning a soft jab in the arm.

"Hey, now," Lucy quipped. "I know what that man did to you in high school. We were all at that graduation party, sweetheart, and the look on your face—"

"Okay, okay," Katie said, holding up her hands in surrender. "We've all made mistakes."

Lucy nodded, a little solemn. "I know, but I always wished he'd show up here again, just so I could kick his ass for you."

Katie couldn't help but laugh at her friend's

loyalty. "You wouldn't hurt a fly, Lucy Haynes."

"You might have a point there, but still, has he talked to you at all?"

Katie took a few steps in silence as they drew closer to the horse stables. "Actually, he's done me one better. He drove me out here after my poor old truck broke down at the pub the other day."

She caught Lucy turning to steal a glance at Ryan. "Well," she said. "If you ask me, he owes you as much."

Katie nodded in agreement. "You're right there, but he's been nothing but an angel since he got here. He and Sarah aren't together anymore, you know. They had their quickie marriage annulled right after they skipped town."

"You're kidding," Lucy said, not even attempting to hide her pleasure at being given this new gossip. Katie and Lucy hadn't exactly been popular in high school, and Ryan Ford, well…was. Katie had never been able to figure out why the older guy was so willing to be followed around by a girl two years younger than him, but Lord, she was glad he had.

"Nope. Cross my heart," Katie said, running her forefinger over her chest in an X shape. "He's a free man."

Lucy looked over at her friend and abruptly stopped walking.

"Oh, my goodness," Lucy said.

"What?"

"Don't you *what* me, Katie Bloom. It's written all over that pretty face of yours, plain as the red in my hair."

Katie still wasn't catching on to what Lucy was talking about.

They were only a few feet away from the

stables when Shiloh drove over in her wheelchair, an excited Shelby on the teenager's lap. Shelby jumped down and ran ahead, pausing to stand at the fence, completely in awe of the two horses visible from where they stood. The child was speechless and Katie knew exactly how she felt, remembering the first time she'd met one of these amazing animals.

"Katie, Katie," Lucy said, "don't you get it? You still like him, don't you?"

Now she had Katie's attention. "Well, of course, I like him. He's always been my best friend. He made a mistake, yes, but he apologized for that and, well, we're working on repairing our friendship."

Lucy shook her head. "No, honey. Not that. I mean in a different way."

Katie felt heat rushing up to her cheeks and Lucy grinned in a knowing way. She'd only just arrived at this information herself…she wasn't sure she was comfortable sharing it with anyone else quite yet. Then again, Lucy was a good friend. She was loyal and could keep things to herself, unlike Katie's very friendly, very chatty grandmother…or June. Katie rolled her eyes. The people of Peach Leaf really needed to give her some space and let her figure this out for herself.

Small towns. Jeez.

"You and June are just…too much."

"What do you mean?"

Katie smiled. "Nothing."

Shelby rejoined them from her perch at the fence, begging Katie and Lucy to introduce her to the large animals, especially a regal-looking white quarter horse she could barely tear her eyes away from.

"Of course, sweetie," Katie said, before

promising to visit with Lucy later. “You sure you don’t want to join us, Luce?” she asked, but her friend waved a hand.

“Nah. I’ll catch up with you later. Maybe we can get together at dinnertime and let Shiloh and Shelby hang out some more.”

Shiloh nodded, smiling at her small friend, and she and Lucy headed back toward the face-painting booth.

“All right, sweetie,” she said, taking Shelby’s fine-boned hand in her own, the smallness of it tickling her heart. Katie had opted out of knowing the sex of her baby, but sometimes she wondered. She would love the child, boy or girl, in equal, overwhelming measure.

She concentrated on Shelby’s joy at meeting the horses, glad for something to distract her from the fear that bubbled up. Her insurance was secure for a full year after the official closure of the museum, as part of the generous severance package she and her coworkers were offered, but after that…

Never mind. She remembered a mantra that she'd first heard from her grandmother as a child. *One day at a time.* It was all she could afford to think about that weekend. There wasn't anything she could do until Monday when she was back in the quiet of home while June worked her shift. She'd get a cup of tea, sit down and start searching for a new job, and she would base her choices on the baby, rather than on finding something she'd really enjoy. This baby would be her life now, and she would do everything in her power to make a good home for him or her…even if that meant the possibility of moving away from Peach Leaf for better work opportunities.

From what she'd gathered listening to folks

around the campground—her coworkers and other townspeople—there was a sense of anticipation about the soon-to-be-built hospital, and in a way she was glad that her friends weren't spending much time mourning the loss of the museum. She knew a cancer treatment center would mean new, welcome job opportunities for the town, but Katie couldn't think of one single thing she'd be qualified for in a place like that.

She'd finished high school and had even taken a few college courses at the community college in Austin, but the living expenses had proved too much and she'd eventually moved home; then she'd met Bradley and moved in with him, found her job, and the rest was history.

Perhaps her grandmother's advice hadn't been the best. Maybe she'd spent so much of her life living one day at a time, and not enough planning for the possibility of her life turning upside down.

She pulled her shoulders down as she led Shelby up to the horse stalls to look on as Alvin, the animals' sweet, gentle caretaker, currycombed a white horse's coat until it shone and studied its tack to check for damage before carefully putting on the saddle pad, saddle and bridle. Then he handed Katie and Shelby each a helmet. Alvin had chosen a sweet, docile horse with no history of throwing off riders for pregnant Katie and her small companion.

He led the horse out of the stables into a small, fenced pasture, holding the reins for Katie as she hoisted herself up and settled into place. As soon as she gave the okay, Alvin lifted Shelby up to her, the little girl's happy squeals chasing away all traces of the anxiety Katie felt only moments ago.

Once they were ready, a helmeted Shelby comfortably and safely in place in front of Katie, the two girls set off down an easy trail.

After about a twenty-minute ride, Katie urged the horse into an easy trot, just to hear Shelby giggle as they bounced along, before dismounting and leading the animal to the river for a quick drink and a few of the chopped carrots Alvin had given Shelby to keep in her pockets. She sat, taking off her shoes and lowering her feet into the water alongside the horse's slurping muzzle, letting the coolness shock her skin. She closed her eyes, enjoying the simple beauty of a happy child and a happy horse.

She heard what sounded like thunder in the distance, but didn't think anything of it, certain it was just the din of enthusiastic people in one place back at camp. But then Shelby tugged at her shirt and she turned to see a rider just over the low hill they'd crossed to reach the water, closing in at a steady pace.

Even though he was too far away for her to see his face, Katie knew instinctively that the black horse's rider was Ryan.

Shelby gave her horse another carrot, delighted when his whiskers tickled her skin, and Katie stole the private moment to enjoy her view as Ryan approached.

He drew nearer and she could see the gilded glow of his hazel eyes, the skin crinkled at their corners with his smile. Katie pulled her feet from the cool water to let them dry, leaning back on her palms, unashamed, to watch as the handsome rider came closer, and closer still, his earnest eyes never leaving hers.

"There're my girls," he said, dismounting before leading the midnight-colored horse to the water next to Shelby's.

Katie's heart lit up at the words. *My girls.* Oh, how she wished it were true for more than that moment.

Something in his face told her that she might not be alone in that desire. Ryan held on to the reins as he sat down next to Katie, letting his horse drink.

"What are you doing out here, cowboy?" she asked, her tone far more flirty than she'd intended. But Ryan didn't laugh as he scooted closer to her.

"Enjoying the fresh air," he said.

"Not a bad idea you've got there." He took off his own shoes and placed his feet in the water. He kicked his foot and a few drops landed on Katie's jeans.

"Hey!" she said, reaching into the water with her hand and returning the splash.

He glanced at Shelby, who'd ignored him in favor of his horse when he'd arrived. The child was happily feeding the new animal the rest of her carrots, her face filled with joy at being the center of two horses' attention. Ryan gave a deep belly laugh, sharing the little girl's delight, then leaned over to whisper in Katie's ear, his warm, peppermint-scented breath causing the little hairs on her neck to stand at attention. "You asked for it," he said, his voice low and sensual. "Sitting there all cute."

Heat bubbled in her abdomen, curling lower as he continued to murmur into her ear, his nose gently grazing the sensitive skin there.

"Do you know what you do to me, Katie?" he asked. "What you've always done to me?"

She shook her head *no*, completely unable to speak.

"I'll tell you soon enough."

Having shocked the absolute tar out of her, Ryan leaned back and gave her a slow, agonizingly gorgeous smile, his eyes glowing like a mischievous panther's in the sunlight, before pulling his feet out of the water. He didn't say a word as he dried them, winking at her as he replaced his socks and got up to join Shelby in feeding snacks to the horses.

She watched him in awe as he laughed with the little girl, treating her as if she was his own and they were out for a day trip as a family.

There it was again—that same thought, the one she'd entertained far too often for her own good that day.

Family.

Part of her wanted to give in to the illusion, to pretend that was what the three of them—Katie, Ryan and Shelby—were, but the other, far wiser part of her knew it was a shaky thing to wish for.

She'd made that mistake before and was still in the process of paying for it, of wondering what her child's life would be like without a father, of wondering if it was her fault, if there was something more she could have done to keep Bradley from leaving, if not for her, then for the sake of their baby.

Katie still couldn't be certain that Ryan was on the same page…or even really what page she was on.

Did she want a relationship with him? Was that really in the best interests of her baby? Even though he'd apologized, and Katie meant what she'd said when she forgave him, was it really wise to let him into her heart again? Into the lives of her and her child? The real question was…could she really risk losing him again?

She wasn't sure that her heart could handle that.

Losing Bradley was one thing, but losing Ryan—again—was something that, she was absolutely certain, had the potential to cause irreparable damage.

She laid a hand on her swollen belly.

Even if she wanted him, and even on the slim chance that he wanted her, too, she owed it to her little one to be cautious, to make every move with both of them in mind. Even if Ryan could be trusted with her heart, there was still so much more she needed to ask him, so much more she needed to find out before she could even begin to think about giving him a single piece of herself.

But for that moment, all she could do was revel in his attention to her, in the way he'd cared for her that day, making sure she'd taken her prenatal vitamins. He'd stopped to buy the three of them breakfast on the way, after finding out that Katie had skipped the meal and chiding her to ensure that she ate regularly that weekend, knowing she'd need the extra energy to keep up with the kids and all of their activities. He'd noticed earlier when she felt a little unbalanced, and had placed a gentle hand under her elbow until she felt steady again. And when she'd suggested that he could head back to town if he needed to, he'd brushed the idea away in a heartbeat, saying something about making sure she had everything she needed and that he'd be there to support her throughout the weekend. Besides, he'd said, he had a hectic week coming up with his work, and he could use a restful weekend before diving into the month ahead.

All outward signs pointed to him being an excellent father, but she still hadn't asked him about his and Sarah's baby.

Something was amiss there, and she needed to find out exactly what it was before she spent another second daydreaming about…about a life with him.

"You ready, Katie?" he asked, holding out a hand to help her up. She accepted his outstretched hand, and although she felt a bit like a beached whale despite being slightly less than halfway through her pregnancy, he lifted her easily off the ground.

It wasn't until she was in a standing position again that a strange feeling hit her.

"Katie? Katie, are you all right?" Ryan asked, his voice sounding farther and farther away as she lost her balance and a strange dizziness engulfed her. Ryan caught her just in time, pulling her against his body to steady her. Shelby wandered over, probably alerted by the worried tone in Ryan's voice.

"Is something wrong, Mr. Ryan?" she asked, folding her hands together in front of her little body. Katie's heart ached at the thought that she'd scared the girl.

"No, sweetie," she said, injecting as much reassurance into her words as possible to calm the sensitive child. "I'm fine."

She looked up at Ryan, whose face was filled with doubt and far more alarm than the situation called for.

"I really am okay," she said, speaking more to him than to Shelby this time. "Just a little dizzy spell is all. I probably haven't had enough water to drink, or need a little more to eat or something. No big deal."

She offered Ryan a reassuring smile and held on to his forearms for a few seconds, making sure that she had her bearings before letting go.

Chapter Nine

Ryan didn't like it one bit.

After what happened to Katie earlier—her sudden, unexplained dizzy spell—he vowed to keep a hawk's eye on her at all times, whether she liked it or not.

And she definitely did not, or so she'd told him in at least ten different ways since they'd returned, wiped down and brushed the horses, and headed over to join the rest of the campers for dinner.

As he grabbed a couple of hot dogs and carelessly doused them with condiments, Ryan watched Katie for any sign of distress. He grabbed an ice-cold Coke from a cooler and walked over to the picnic table where she sat, her flushed face shielded from the sun by a canopy. She looked a little tired but happy as she laughed at something Liam and Paige Campbell's little boy said and helped Shelby cut up her food.

His heart lifted a little, seeing Katie next to the sweet little girl he'd only met that morning. He wondered if the baby he and Sarah had lost—the little girl he'd never known but loved with no less ferocity—would have become anything like Shelby.

He'd had some time to heal after the stillbirth, and when he took a hard look at the situation, he knew that he didn't really miss

Sarah. What he missed was what she'd represented: family. The possibility of home and all that meant. He'd wanted so badly for it to work out between them, all the while knowing that his heart didn't belong to her. It belonged to Katie—always had, always would.

He never should have tried to pretend otherwise.

He knew things were over with Sarah before she gave birth to a baby that wasn't breathing. Sarah knew it, too. They'd discussed the possibility of annulment a few times during her pregnancy, but Ryan had always refused. He wouldn't be like his father. He would be someone they could rely on and trust. Even if things weren't perfect with Sarah, he'd promised to always be there...a promise he'd taken very seriously.

But after what happened, after they'd tried

to help each other through the crippling grief, Sarah had called it quits, and Ryan, weary from sorrow and the truth of what his life had become, had agreed. They parted amicably and checked in on each other now and then. They would always share a sort of bond, but they would never love each other.

Strange, he thought, how trying so hard to be a good man…to be honest and true and loyal…had turned him into a liar.

The only truth he'd ever known for certain was that he loved Katie Bloom.

And it was also the only truth he'd never spoken out loud.

He would have to change that, and soon. He would have to face his fear—the very real possibility that she did not feel the same, at least not anymore—and tell her what had been in his heart for so long.

The day away from his father, from their work on the hospital blueprints, was a good thing for him. He'd spent so long hiding in his work the past few years, and it was a little strange to be experiencing something else, something entirely unrelated to his business. It reminded him that there were more important things in life than work and that he really should try to find some balance.

Katie looked up when he sat next to her on the picnic table bench, her dark eyes more alive than they'd been earlier. Perhaps she was right and it was only a benign dizzy spell, and she just needed to eat something and get a little more water into her system.

"Hey, you," she said, her smooth voice soothing his worry a little bit. "We were wondering what you'd gotten into."

He greeted the Campbells and tucked into his food.

"You know how Peach Leaf is. Everyone wants to know where I've been and what I've been up to. It's like if I haven't been here, I must have just fallen off the face of the Earth or something."

She made a chiding sound. "They're just curious and they care about you." She stabbed a piece of salad greens with her fork and took a bite. "We all do."

They spent the rest of dinner together, and Ryan felt the good company and good food spread over him like a salve. Watching the sun set over rolling hills, its fading beams of light stretching out over the river's clear blue water in the distance, he let thoughts of work slip away, allowing himself to soak up the comfort and familiarity of being home.

And then, finally, it was time for everyone's favorite part of the entire day.

Katie's excitement was contagious, spreading through everyone around her as she helped set up for the hayride. While most of the families relaxed and let their bellies settle after dinner, Ryan and the other guys used pitchforks to transfer hay that had been dropped off near the barn into a few of their trucks. Katie wanted to help, of course, but Ryan wouldn't allow it, promising that if she'd just keep her hands off anything heavy and let him do all the lifting, then she could have the pleasure of keeping him company in his truck through the rides.

Katie laughed, the last shreds of sunshine bouncing off her cheekbones, illuminating her long, dark hair like a halo.

"Someone thinks awful highly of himself," she teased, and Ryan felt heat fill his face.

Damn, he loved her flirting.

The sound of her voice and the sultry undertone lacing her words resurrected a part of Ryan that he'd thought long dead. Being with Katie, especially this Katie, the bold, brave Katie standing in front of him now—the one he hadn't realized he'd missed so much until he'd stepped back into her life—made him feel alive again.

"You're the one I think highly of, Katie," he said, and the complete honesty of his words didn't even surprise him. She had that effect on him. It was an inexplicable power she held over him. He couldn't go long without being himself around her, without being completely open and exposed.

He wasn't much good at emotional stuff,

but it was almost as if…they were meant to be in close proximity to each other, as if they couldn't be wholly themselves apart from the other.

Even a few days ago, he would have expected such a thought to freak him out, but now, being with her in a place they'd always loved, a place where they'd spent so much of the best parts of childhood, it seemed almost natural that they would come together again.

His words must have awakened something inside her because the next thing he knew, she'd stepped closer and closer until she was almost in his arms, and then…she was. And in the next instant, she'd laced her fingers around his neck and pulled his face down until he could feel the soft warmth of her breath on his chin.

He wanted to kiss her with every nerve in

his body, and it took a mighty force to keep him from doing just that. He didn't even care that several pairs of eyes were on them, that some of the other adults had stopped what they were doing to prep for the hayride, in favor of focusing on him and Katie.

"Do you really mean that?" she said softly, the sound of her voice causing his pulse to speed up.

Keeping a hold on his racing heart, on the ache building in his groin, he wrapped his arms around her waist, still careful to maintain some distance between them. There were kids around, after all, he reminded himself, so he couldn't give in to his impulse and lower her into the hay to make love to her underneath the setting sun. He'd have to keep it together.

Plus, there were things they needed to

address before he would allow himself to let go. There were things the two of them needed to talk about, things he had to say to Katie before they could be together…if that was what she wanted.

All signs pointed to yes. The dilated pupils making her eyes almost black, the tiny tap dance he could see her pulse doing in that soft spot near her ear and the raw heat that filled up the ever-decreasing space between them.

It was almost too much. The urge to have his mouth on hers was no longer tolerable, so he pulled away, instantly greeted by clear disappointment in her expression.

"I do mean it, Katie. More than you know, but we need to talk. That is—" he stared straight into the seemingly endless depths of her eyes "—I need some time alone with you."

She nodded in agreement but he could see

that she was deeply affected by the quick separation of their bodies. He regretted causing the sad look in her eyes, but if he was going to give his heart to Katie Bloom, it would be with no strings attached, with everything on the table. He needed to know what was going on in her life, what had happened to the father of her baby, before he'd give her his heart.

Because when he did, when he knew where she stood and if she was on board, he would give her everything. And it would be the last time.

So it had to be right. It had to be perfect.

And there might be a little pain to get through first.

Katie brushed hair away from her face and stepped a few feet away, her hands on her hips, making her seem nervous or irritated. Ryan wanted to comfort her, but the kids were gathering around, eager to pile into the truck and circle around the campground. He focused on the hayride to get the awkward moment with Katie out of his mind. It was such a simple thing, dried-up grass in an old truck bed and, honestly, a pretty boring loop of dirt road, but even Ryan had to admit it was a heck of a lot of fun. Even though their parents had always tagged along to help chaperone the trip, he and Katie had looked forward to the half hour out of their sight to tell ghost stories in the back of a pickup, the stars overhead the only source of light.

Ryan and Katie and the other adults helped the kids get settled and tossed a couple of blankets into the back of the truck in case anyone got chilly in the crisp, late-October air, and then Ryan opened his passenger door and helped Katie up into the cab. They'd reassured

Shelby that she could join them if she wanted to, but to everyone's joy, the little girl's earlier shyness seemed to have passed, and she wanted to ride in the back with the rest of the kids, provided Ryan and Katie promised to take care of Jeff in the front seat.

They agreed, and Katie happily settled the turtle on the seat between them, buckling in his little plastic shelter for good measure, checking for Shelby's seal of approval.

After a bout of rain the week before, the skies were clear as could be, casting the perfect backdrop for the millions of stars twinkling overhead. Ryan rolled down the windows before starting up the truck. The kids in the back squealed with glee and Katie, having forgotten the uneasiness of their moment earlier, bounced up and down in her seat to Ryan's delight.

Nothing made him happier than seeing her so happy, he realized.

If she'd let him, when the time was right, he would offer everything in his power to do that very thing for the rest of their lives.

The silence in the truck with Ryan was so deafening that Katie could barely think, still reeling from their almost-kiss.

She hadn't felt so alive since she'd found out she was pregnant, and even then, the news had been bittersweet, given Bradley's reaction.

What was going on with Ryan was different, amazing…terrifying.

Each moment they spent together was filled with an electric buzz of tension that she knew they could both feel, but then Ryan would pull back, almost as though he was afraid to acknowledge what was going on between them.

When she'd seen him across the room a few days ago at the pub, she'd walked out, completely committed to the idea of not facing their past and never seeing him again.

But now…now she couldn't even imagine, could barely remember what life was like without him. He'd arrived so suddenly, his presence shocking to her system at the time, but since then, he'd filled almost every crack in her world.

Yeah, she still didn't have a job to go back to, and there was the baby to worry about, but for some reason, a reason she didn't even need to understand, Ryan made all of that seem small in comparison to the raw desire that overcame her when he drew near.

All she knew was that she wanted more of him, but every time they got close to giving in to what they both wanted, he pulled away again.

"Ryan," she said, her voice coming out too loud in the silent car, "what happened back there?"

His eyes remained on the road as he drove through the night, the soft hum of the parents in the back telling the kids ghost stories seeming far away. Katie couldn't tell what was going through his mind, but she wanted to draw near, to comfort him with her warm body.

But not quite enough to risk getting pushed away again.

"I told you about Sarah," he said softly, his voice tight with emotion, "but I didn't tell you the reason I'm back in town."

It was true. She'd been wondering off and

on, but the heightening awareness of their attraction had distracted her from finding out.

"I just assumed you were here to visit your parents," she said, giving him the only reason she could think of for his appearance in Peach Leaf. Part of her wished he'd come back just to make amends with her, just to tell her… what? That he wanted to be with her? That he wanted their friendship back?

"That's part of it, but there is more," he said, his hands gripping the steering wheel so tight that his knuckles were white.

"Well, tell me, then," she said.

He pulled in a deep breath, letting the air out slowly as she waited.

"I'm part of the reason the museum is shutting down."

His words didn't make sense, didn't explain what he meant.

"What do you mean?" she asked, confused. "My boss told me that the museum is being razed to make room for a hospital."

"Cancer treatment facility," Ryan corrected. "And your boss is absolutely correct."

Katie still didn't understand. "What does that have to do with you being back in town?"

"My architecture firm in Seattle was hired on to take care of the planning aspect of the job—the blueprints and development of the building."

It made sense now. Katie had known that Ford Construction was the builder and that Ryan's dad would be in charge. And she could only assume that Ryan had studied architecture in college, because it had always been his dream—he'd always had an incredible talent for taking things apart and putting them back together in ways that improved them—

but until he'd spoken the words out loud, she hadn't put two and two together.

"Oh," she said, her voice gravelly like the road beneath the truck's tires, "I see."

Her heart was pounding as she tried to make sense of things, to put all the pieces together to form something whole and comprehendible.

"Did you know about the museum getting torn down when you signed on for the job?"

He didn't answer her, but when he briefly glanced at her before turning back to the road, she saw all she needed to.

"You did, didn't you?"

"Yes, Katie," he said, an urgency in his voice. "But I had no idea you worked there. If I'd known, I might have—"

She held up a hand.

"You might have what?"

She wanted him to say he would have reconsidered, but he didn't…just let her question hang in the air.

She shook her head and gave a pained chuckle. "It doesn't matter anyway. Even if I didn't work there, it's still a major thing for this town."

"Yeah, I know that, I do." He hesitated before continuing, "But so is the cancer center. It will mean a great deal to a lot of people. It means better health care, better treatment for a disease that affects so many and more jobs—"

"What about my job?" she asked, her voice quiet but tinged with emotion. She didn't want him to see that this was hurting her, but it was, and she couldn't hide it anymore. She'd tried for the past few days to keep positive, both for her own good and for everyone else's. It seemed everyone was trying to just ignore the inevitable—they were all trying to enjoy their last Pumpkin Fest without talking about the elephant in the room, but Katie couldn't hold back any longer.

"You'll find something else, Katie. You're an intelligent, hardworking woman, and everybody in Peach Leaf knows that. No one will hesitate to give you a new job."

"That might be true if there were jobs to be had, Ryan, but things are slow to recover from economic blows in a small town. You might have forgotten that when you moved away to Seattle, but that's how it goes for those of us who stayed."

She took a deep breath to calm down, focusing her attention out the window, taking a moment to slow her heart rate and to try to enjoy the last few miles of what could be her last Pumpkin Fest hayride.

When she spoke again, her head was clearer,

and she knew better what she wanted to say. "I know the cancer facility will offer more jobs, and I know it's a good thing for the town. I do. But—" she choked up "—but the museum is important, too. At least, it is to me. I worked there for five years, Ryan. I started as a ticket seller and now I'm teaching and directing programs. And I'm about to be a mom."

She closed her eyes and squeezed them tight, willing away tears. "I'm in no position to start all over at another job."

"I know it is," he said, looking at her again, his hazel eyes full of emotion. "And I do care about that, more than you know."

He reached over to lay his large, strong hand over hers, the feel of his skin distracting her from her agitation.

"I grew up in this town, too, Katie. I'll miss

the museum, the Pumpkin Fest and the hay-rides, too."

Tears welled up in her eyes and she turned back to the window to keep him from seeing them fall.

"And even though they'll be farther away, the artifacts, the buildings will all be kept safe and you can visit them when you want."

Katie wiped her eyes. Maybe she was being silly by trying to hold on to the past.

"You don't need to worry about a job, either, Katie. I'll make sure you're taken care of… whether that means finding you a position at the center or something else."

His voice sounded rocky when he spoke the last part of that sentence, and if she'd been able to speak without her voice breaking, she might have asked what he meant. She did not want a job that she didn't earn herself, but she had the baby to care for, so she might not have a choice.

"I'd really prefer not to have to take a charity job," she said, her voice thankfully solid, brushing over her next unspoken words—*though I will if I have to.*

Ryan's mouth, the one she'd almost kissed only a half hour earlier, curved at the corners in a sexy grin. "You always were stubborn as an ox, Katie Bloom," he said.

She wasn't going to let him off the hook that easily. Katie would not lightly accept any attempt on his part to secure her a job, and she would not allow him to use the pull of his family name to make the situation easier on her than it would be for her coworkers and friends who would lose their jobs when the museum closed. She didn't want Ryan Ford's help. There was plenty she did want from him, she'd realized over the past few days, but that wasn't part of it.

When they returned from the hayride, Katie let Ryan help her out of the truck, then handed over Jeff the turtle to take inside the cabin. A hint of the dizziness she'd felt earlier returned briefly, but luckily Ryan didn't notice and it passed while he helped the kids and parents out of the back of his truck.

The sight of him holding a sleeping Shelby brought back some of the tears she'd shed earlier, and she thought again of how hard it would be on the girl to return to the children's home the next day. She made a mental note to visit more often in the coming weeks to make sure Shelby was okay, especially since she would soon have more time on her hands.

When everyone was safely out of the trucks and into the cabins for the night, Katie was finally able to relax a little. She helped Shelby brush her teeth despite the child's drowsiness, and they made it through only half of one of the bedtime stories Katie had promised earlier to read. She tucked the little girl in tight before brushing her own teeth and returning to sit on the edge of her bottom bunk. She said good-night to Paige, Lucy, Shiloh and some of the other women and tried for a little while to sleep before eventually giving up, knowing her dreams would be filled with Ryan Ford.

Chapter Ten

The pull of the clear night sky and the cool air drew her out of her bed a few hours later, and she shoved her feet into flip-flops, wrapping her robe around her shoulders. Lucy was propped up in her top bunk over Shiloh, reading with a book light, and Katie stopped to tell her friend that she'd be right back—she just needed to step out for some fresh air.

"Are you sure you're okay?" Lucy asked, her forehead creasing with worry.

Katie waved a hand, brushing off the other woman's concern. "Yeah, I'm fine. I just need a minute to myself after all the chaos."

Lucy smiled and, after further reassurance from Katie, returned to her book.

Katie grabbed her cell phone and turned on the flashlight app as she walked outside.

The night was gorgeous, and she stared up at the stars as she wandered the grounds, no real goal in mind of where she might want to go. She passed the guys' cabin and couldn't keep from wondering if Ryan was in bed, able to sleep far better than her. Their earlier conversation still weighed on Katie's mind, and no matter how much she paced, it wouldn't go away. She thought of him as she snuck some apples from the kitchen to feed the horses, and even letting them tickle her palm with their noses didn't ease her stress.

Eventually, she meandered down to the river, slipping off her flip-flops to let her feet soak in the cool water like she had earlier when she'd ridden out to the stream with Shelby and Ryan…

"Is there room at all in your thoughts for me?"

Katie wasn't even startled at the sound of Ryan's voice. Maybe she'd heard his footsteps drawing up the soft dirt path behind her, or maybe she just wasn't at all surprised that he'd come out to find her.

But his statement rattled her to the bone. "Quite the opposite, actually," she said, turning her head to the side, unable to see him in the darkness. "There doesn't seem to be room for much else at the moment."

She was glad for the lack of light, glad that the cover of night hid all the emotions whirling around inside her from being visible on her face.

It seemed like several moments passed, and Ryan didn't speak. She was glad he didn't try to fill the silence. It was possible they'd spoken too much that day, shared too much of themselves with each other, and now it was time to let the quiet talk for them.

The next thing she knew, Ryan had lowered himself to the ground to sit behind her, and suddenly his firm chest was against her back, his legs curved around hers. He breathed in deeply, his nose tucked into her hair, and then set his chin on top of her head, wrapping his arms around her, settling them atop her belly.

She could barely breathe, her body so full of longing, of confusion and of desire for him that she just sat there, unable to think or move at all.

Finally, she lifted her hands from her lap to hold his arms, and they sat there like that, silent in the darkness, for a long time.

"Katie," Ryan said, his voice barely audible, hardly more than a whisper in the cool night air. "My mom has cancer. When my dad invited me to design the new cancer treatment hospital for his company, I took the job because I couldn't turn down such a great project for my firm. But then I found out that my dad had a deeper reason for building the facility…Mom. And now it's my reason, too."

Katie sucked in air and closed her eyes as the pain in his words hit her in the center of her heart. She'd been so focused on her own issues earlier, on worrying about how the museum's closure would affect her and her friends, that she hadn't even stopped to consider that Ryan might have his own reasons for the project.

Of course he did, though. Of course Ryan Ford had a good cause for helping his father. That was who Ryan was. He didn't do things haphazardly or without logic and thought. He was a good, good man—she'd always known that, even when she'd watched him drive away from her that night and out of her life. He always had others' best interests in mind in every move he made. She'd been so blind to that fact before, so selfish. How badly he must be hurting to be dealing alone with his mother's illness, and to have agreed to work with a man with whom, Ryan had explained earlier, he was on shaky ground.

"Oh, Ryan," she said, holding tighter to his arms, curling her fingers into his warm skin. "I'm so, so sorry."

"It's okay," he said, moving his head to tuck his chin into the curve between her shoulder and ear. She leaned her face against his, felt a tear fall from her eye onto his cheek.

"Hey, hey," he said softly, "It's okay."

Katie could hear his voice falter and knew his words were as much for himself as they were for her. Suddenly she knew she would do anything, would move Heaven and Earth, to make him feel better…if only she knew what that was.

"Is there anything I can do to…help?" she asked, her own voice shaking.

"You're doing it now," he answered.

"What do you mean?"

"Shh, Katie," he said. "Just let me hold you." He wrapped his arms tighter around her; it felt simultaneously natural and earth-shattering to be held by him. For the longest time, she'd thought she was just lost without him, that she'd never be able to find someone like him again. She'd settled for Bradley, had done her best with their relationship, knowing all the time, somewhere in the very back of her mind, that he wasn't The One.

It was Ryan. It was always Ryan.

Why had it taken her so long to come to that seemingly obvious conclusion?

"I've wanted to do this for so long," Ryan said, and she could feel his desire for her as he pulled her in even closer. "I've wanted to know what it would be like to feel you against my body, to have you this close to me."

Katie closed her eyes, letting a moment she'd always wanted wash over her.

"I wanted you to be my first, Katie, but I didn't think you'd ever feel the same way, so when Sarah came along, I just..."

It was her turn to silence him, so she did, turning her body so that she faced Ryan. She reached up and placed her palms on either side of his gorgeous face—a face forever etched into her brain—and studied the way starlight danced in his hazel eyes, the way his lips looked, slightly parted, waiting for hers. And then she pulled him to her face and pressed her lips over his, the contact pulsing from where their mouths touched all the way to her toes. He kissed her back with greater urgency, gently moving her lips apart with his tongue, pressing his mouth harder against hers and exploring deeper, deeper, until neither of them could breathe.

When they were both so full of need that it was obvious they wouldn't be able to keep their hands off each other for much longer, Katie pulled away and stood up, leaving a perplexed Ryan on the ground behind her. He grinned up at her, eyes full of boyish mischief, and then he was off the ground, too, chasing her as she jogged gently, careful to watch her steps, along the river's edge, both wanting him to catch her and uncertain of what might happen if he did.

They were kids again, and it was just another Pumpkin Fest at the campground, Ryan and Katie laughing and playing tag in the darkness after sneaking out of their cabins. It was so familiar...but everything was different.

They were grown-ups now, with heartaches, responsibilities, bills...but something new, too. They'd crossed over a seemingly unsurpassable hill. She had always been afraid of what it would be like on this side—what it would be like for Ryan to know how she felt about him—and she'd always worried that he would scoff at her or run from her or...who knew what else.

But now, even though she hadn't really said the words...somehow he knew what was in her heart, and instead of running away, he was chasing her.

Katie smiled, slowing to a stop at the water's edge, the craziness of the past few days and the protection of the darkness's cloak making her braver than she'd ever felt before. Without a hint of shyness, she began to pull off her clothing, one item at a time. She didn't even have to turn around to know that she had Ryan in her spell. She could feel energy coming from where he stood about ten feet away, watching as she undressed, the only illumination coming from the soft glow cast by the moon.

Off went her long-sleeved shirt and the last

pair of non-maternity jeans in her closet that still fit. She reached around and unsnapped her bra, still facing the river so that Ryan couldn't see all of her, and, finally, biting her lip and suddenly wondering if she was crazy-high on pregnancy hormones, she shucked her panties, tossing them on the ground behind her.

Without a stitch of clothing left, she turned and glanced over her shoulder, meeting Ryan's eyes in the moonlight, her long hair grazing her back. Her eyes invited—dared—him to join her, and she didn't even stop to think about whether the water might be turning cold, the last warm days of summer not hot enough in the daytime to heat it, and she started running.

Katie ran until she reached the water's edge, then plunged in, the sharp coolness temporarily shocking the wind out of her until she laughed and drew a deep breath. She began to tread water and got her bearings just in time to see Ryan following her motions.

She'd always known his body would be toned—he'd always loved sports and played something or other every season—and man, was she right. Splinters of light bounced off his hard chest as he pulled his shirt over his head and threw it to the side, followed by his jeans, displaying muscular thighs underneath his boxers. Up until then, she'd been grateful for the black cover of night, but now she cursed it, wishing she could see every inch of him in the full light of day.

He didn't shed the shorts as he walked toward the water.

"Not fair," she said, teasing him as he came closer to the river.

"If you want to play games, you'd better think about the rules before you get started," he said in answer.

She tilted her head to the side, enjoying watching the way his body moved under the glinting light as he sauntered toward her with the confident grace of a panther.

"All right, then," she said, taking the bait. "Rule number one—no going *all the way.*" Katie grinned. "There are kids here."

Ryan put a hand under his chin, considering. "Says the naked woman in the river."

"We're far enough from the cabins that no one can see me. And all the girls were asleep when I left except Lucy, who had her nose in a book," she reasoned.

"Deal," he said, "but only while we're here." He crouched down and Katie swam over until their noses touched. "Once I get you back to town, I make no promises to keep that one."

"Fair enough," she acquiesced, weaving her arms through the water to keep afloat. "Your turn."

"Rule number two," Ryan said. "No swimming away from me once I get into the water. You're to stay put."

"And why is that?" Katie asked, feigning bewilderment.

Ryan put his palms behind him onshore, sliding into the water with an agonizing lack of speed. Katie's pulse was pounding so hard she could barely focus as he sidled up next to her, his height such that he could touch the bottom of the river, leaving her vulnerable. She gasped and lost her balance when he reached out to her, slipping his hands around her middle to pull her near, pressing her full breasts against his naked skin. The connection set off an ache between her legs, which grew progressively excruciating when he kissed her. Her body went limp in his arms, and his desire for her was undeniable.

"So I can touch every inch of you without you getting away from me," he said before nibbling on her lip. Katie was helpless at his touch as he moved one arm to caress her back, settling a hand under her bottom to hold her in place while his mouth took hers once again.

He pulled away so suddenly that she gave a little moan of protest. "What's rule number three?" he asked.

She pulled in air, struggling to catch her breath. "Rule number three," she whispered into his ear. "Don't let go."

And with that, she kissed him again and again until they couldn't stand it anymore.

When it became too much, Katie wriggled out of Ryan's arms and swam off, following the moonlight's reflection on the water until she was out of his reach. He trailed closely behind until she stopped to face him again, and they splashed each other all the way back to shore, only to swim out again, remembering what it was like to feel like kids, taking back what they'd lost.

They swam for hours, teasing each other, reveling in the new feeling of their mouths together, their skin floodlit by the moon and stars. And when they were too tired to swim any longer, Ryan dried off Katie's body, inch by inch, and tugged on his clothes before lifting her into his arms. He carried her closer to the cabins and lit a campfire in the pit outside, wrapping a blanket around her shoulders, and held her close by the firelight.

Katie wasn't sure whether the warmth coming from Ryan's body or that of the flames was what finally melted away all her cares, but she drifted off into a deep sleep.

They woke in each other's arms, sunlight washing over their skin as dawn stretched into morning. The first thing Katie saw when she opened her eyes was Ryan's face—that face she'd loved since they were children. She reached up to touch him, memorizing every inch—just in case she never got another chance—before pulling herself away. Katie tucked the flannel blanket over his chest and shoulders and up underneath his chin, escaping into her cabin before the night had a chance to catch up with her.

The ride back to Peach Leaf the next day was the longest of Ryan's life. All he could think about was the way Katie had looked the night before, her chocolate eyes glimmering in the darkness, communicating her desire far better than any words could, and the way her skin had warmed under his palms as he'd slid his hands against her body, using touch to drink in the curves he couldn't see in the darkness.

It had taken all his might not to pull her out of the river and take her right there on the bank, but, like Katie, when the moment came, he wanted to know they were completely alone to explore each other fully, without another care in the world.

He kept his eyes on the road as they drove, focusing his attention on Shelby and her turtle in the seat next to him, rather than on the ache he would feel when they parted ways. He'd already begun to plan, to consider the logistics of adopting the girl, but he wasn't sure the agency would be too keen on giving her up to a single guy with a demanding, full-time job.

He would speak to Katie's grandmother on Monday and see if she could pull any strings to convince whoever was in charge that he would make a damn good father. And he would. Of that, he was certain. Sarah's stillbirth had completely crushed him. He'd been terrified, yes, only eighteen at the time, working two jobs to pay for college after being denied help from his father. On those stressful nights when he should have been sleeping, his thoughts had been occupied with worry about how he would support his young family. But none of that could do anything to change the way he felt about that baby. He'd wanted to meet her so badly, had looked forward to the day when he'd see her little face, and his heart had broken when she'd made her way into the world, pale blue and tiny…too late for anyone to save her.

After things ended with Sarah, he'd poured his grief into finishing school and working his way up at a firm under the guidance of a good mentor who'd helped him get a loan when he was ready to start his own business.

Eventually, when he'd had money and a little extra time, he'd found a solid therapist, who helped him work through the guilt he carried at being unable to save his own baby…a daughter whose face was so incredibly beautiful, her expression oddly at peace despite her early entrance into the world.

It still amazed him how much he'd loved someone he had never had a chance to know.

Shelby reminded him so much of that little

girl. His heart lurched every time he looked at the sweet person Katie had introduced him to only the day before.

Somehow he managed to keep his cool when they dropped Shelby off at the children's home, as much for Katie as himself. He knew her hormones were a little shaky with her pregnancy, and he didn't want her to have any reason to get upset when they said goodbye.

Somewhere inside, he could almost see a family forming right there in his reach—him, Shelby, Katie and her little one—that was close enough to touch, if only he would take it.

Before they left the facility, he pulled Katie's grandmother aside to speak to her alone, and she promised to get the ball rolling to gather the adoption paperwork, unable to stop smiling. He asked her to keep this from Katie as long as possible. If things didn't work out, and he knew there was a strong likelihood of that, there wasn't any point in them both suffering disappointment. It would be his secret with Mrs. Bloom for now, and he would tell Katie when the time was right…after he told her that he was falling for her more and more each day.

Chapter Eleven

The next night, Katie checked her appearance one last time, noting how much different things were now than the last time she'd taken a shower there, waiting for Ryan to show up at her door. She'd spent extra time curling her long hair until it hung down her back in soft waves, and her lips had curved in a helpless smile as she'd donned the necklace with a dragonfly pendant that her mother gave her on her sixteenth birthday.

It was so strange to think that Ryan would see it tonight, an object he'd looked upon a hundred times before, in a completely different way.

She imagined what it would be like when the evening wore on and it was just the two of them, Katie wearing only the necklace.

Her heart skipped a beat and she felt her cheeks warm at the images in her mind. It had taken her the entire drive home to get over the fact that she'd behaved so completely absurdly with Ryan the night before at the river. It wasn't like her to be so bold, to take risks like that with her image…or her heart. She knew he would never say a word about it to anyone—it would remain between them—yet it still had the power to make her blush.

Not that he'd complained.

She'd seen the way his eyes lit up when

he'd stared at the few parts of her naked body he'd been able to see in the darkness, and she couldn't wait to see them canvass her that night.

She swiped on lipstick and turned out the bathroom light, nearly bumping into June as she stepped into the hallway.

"Nosy Rosy," she said, poking June in her ribs.

June only shrugged. "My dating life sucks. I have to live vicariously through you."

Katie rolled her eyes. "Your dating life does not suck," she said.

"That's because it doesn't exist," June answered, crossing her arms over her chest as she admired Katie's outfit, one she'd helped pick.

"You look amazing, by the way," she said, letting out a whistle.

Katie did a little spin. "All thanks to you, my friend."

June gave her a hug. "I told you this would happen, didn't I?"

"Nothing's happened yet," Katie said, crossing to her room to grab her purse. "It's just dinner, that's all."

"I can only hope not."

They burst into laughter, only stopping at the sound of the doorbell.

"That's him," Katie said. "Wish me luck."

"No need," June said, her confident voice boosting Katie's nerves a little. "In that dress, he'll be unable to resist you."

"After this long," Katie replied, "he'd better not."

She headed to answer the door, and the sight of Ryan dressed up took her breath away as he grabbed her hand and led her to his truck.

He took her to one of the fanciest places in town, a gorgeous Italian restaurant on Main Street—one she'd never been able to afford on her own. She'd admired the menu in passing on more than one occasion, stopping to stare at the delicious-looking dishes on her way from the museum to her car.

She hoped she'd dressed up enough for the little bistro in a black dress that was a little more revealing than the clothes she usually wore. Looking down, she could see a hint of cleavage, one of the perks of pregnancy being that her chest was slightly more ample than its usual state. June had assured Katie that she looked great and that she was being overly modest.

Little did she know that Katie had very recently performed quite the striptease down to nothing, outdoors no less.

Her heels weren't too high—her ankles were a little swollen lately—and she'd brought a wrap in case the weather got a little chilly.

All in all, she felt pretty damn good.

"You're beautiful, Katie Bloom," Ryan said the minute they were seated, giving her a gorgeous, dimpled smile over the light of the candle in a green bottle between them.

She thanked him and busied herself with the menu, suddenly feeling a little shy, despite what they'd now been through together. After narrowing her choices down to three entrées, an almost impossible feat in itself, Katie ordered gnocchi served with shrimp, asparagus and pesto. The waiter complimented her choice in a wonderfully thick, Italian accent and took her menu, turning to Ryan, who requested a smoked-salmon dish for himself, and an antipasto plate of artichoke hearts, sliced tomatoes marinated in dressing, thinly sliced Genoa salami and Cacio de Roma cheese, shaved prosciutto and crusty bread for he and Katie to share.

The food was so good that there was little room for talking, and it wasn't until her belly was full of deliciousness that Katie noticed Ryan was studying her, face resting on his palms over his empty plate.

"What?" she asked, nervously wiping her mouth. "Do I have food on my face?"

He gave a low, sexy laugh. "No, not at all. I'm just happy to be sitting here with you."

She put down her napkin and folded her hands in her lap. "Me, too," she said, a wide, genuine smile breaking open on her face.

He had a way of making her feel unselfconscious, unafraid to be herself in his presence, and she loved him for that.

The word jolted her. Actually, she loved him for a lot of things.

If only it were that easy to just tell him.

"Ryan—" she started, at the same time as he said her name, causing them both to laugh.

"It should be easier, huh?" he said, his frank honesty disarming her a little.

"Do you think that means something?" she asked, worried about his reply.

He waited for the waiter to clear their table, ordering a dessert of Italian cream cake for them to share.

"I don't think it's ever easy," he said, taking a sip of his wine, "when two people who have known each other for so long dare to turn their friendship into something new. I think it can be scary…I know I feel that way…but I don't think that's unusual, no."

His openness gave her the doorway she

needed to tell him what she'd been holding back. She was certain he'd wondered about her baby, about his or her father, but he'd been so patient in waiting for her to talk about it.

It was time.

"His name is Bradley," Katie said. "The father." She glanced up to check Ryan's expression, calmed by the easy smile she was met with.

"I had been wondering," he said, and she giggled.

"You don't have to talk about him if you don't want to, Katie," he said, giving her an out that she wouldn't take. She was thankful for it all the same.

"No," she said, "it's okay. We broke up when I found out about the baby."

Ryan placed his hands on the table, gripping the cloth. "He left you because of the baby?"

Truthfully, Katie was flattered by his reaction. Ryan was protective and strong in ways Bradley never had been—one of the many flaws she'd chosen to overlook in her ex because it was easier than fighting with him.

"Well, it wasn't just that," she said.

"He did, didn't he?" Ryan shook his head. "What a bastard."

"We had other problems," Katie continued.

"It doesn't matter," he said. "He shouldn't have left you alone and pregnant. He should have stayed to take care of you…to be a father to his kid."

Katie fiddled with her napkin, searching for the best response. "Well, first of all, not everyone is as good a man as you are, Ryan Ford—" she pointed her gaze at him— "and second, it's not always that simple."

Though, she knew, to Ryan, it really was.

Wasn't he the one who'd rushed into marrying his high school girlfriend after discovering that he was going to be a dad?

He'd always seen the world in black and white; it was why he had such a hard time with the idea of forgiving his father. Katie didn't know the specifics of the situation, but from what he'd shared before, it seemed like a fairly dramatic affair for their family. She remembered how Ryan's mom used to look at her husband—with such blatant adoration—and she'd always believed it was reciprocated. They were a beautiful couple, and she was still sad after hearing what happened to their marriage, though it happened years ago and they were still together. Maybe they'd been able to repair the damage Mr. Ford had caused.

If his mother had been able to forgive him,

then Ryan needed to find a way to do so, as well. There was no excuse for what the man had done, but it would only hurt Ryan to hold a grudge.

"Not everyone has your hero-style moral code, Ryan, though the world would probably be a better place if more people did."

Her last comment elicited a grin from him, as she'd hoped. The light moment passed and she became serious again. "There were things that were my fault, too," she said. "Really, Ryan, I'm not perfect."

"Could have fooled me," he said, reaching across the table to hold her hand.

She let the sensation of his skin on hers comfort her.

"One of our problems was that Bradley was never going to be right for me."

Candlelight flickered in Ryan's hazel eyes.

"Because I was always still in love with someone else."

Katie saw her own expression reflected in Ryan's, and he seemed about to say something else when their dessert arrived. They dug into the fluffy white cake, remarking on the absolute perfection of coconut and pecan, leaving the restaurant in a haze of sweetness.

An hour later, Ryan led Katie up to his hotel room, her hand in his as they rode the elevator to his suite on the top floor.

They didn't speak as he took her wrap and bag, hanging them on a coatrack by the door, before leading her to the bedroom. At the river, they'd been playful, but somehow Katie knew that when Ryan made love with her, it wouldn't be with a light heart. He would be a completely present lover, all of his attention focused solely on his partner…on her.

She excused herself and went into the en suite bathroom, laying her hands on either side of the sink to catch her breath. She'd waited for this moment since she'd realized her deep attraction for her best friend, and now that it was here, so many things were flooding her mind that she needed a minute to clear her head.

Katie splashed water on her face, set her shoulders back and returned to the bedroom, where Ryan stood near the window, looking out over their hometown. He turned when he felt her reenter the room, but he didn't say a word. Just let his eyes linger on every part of her…face, breasts, belly, legs…before he crossed the room in a few long steps, taking her hands in his to lead her to the bed.

Katie sat on the edge and pulled off her shoes; Ryan did the same before sitting down, patting the spot next to him, indicating that she should come closer.

"Fine pair, the two of us," he said, reaching forward to run a finger down Katie's arm, shoulder to wrist. "We're both so hardheaded and stubborn that we went off and made a mess of our lives with other people, too blind to know that we had the best person right there in front of us, all the time. Or at least I did."

His touch was electric and she nearly missed what he'd said.

Part of her wanted him to continue speaking, but another part—the part that won—wanted so badly for him to hold her again like he had in the river, to feel his large, strong hands on every hill and valley of her body. When he'd kissed her the day before, he'd awoken an appetite she'd never known before, and now she needed that physical contact like water and sun, nourishment that only Ryan could provide.

She took his hand when it reached hers and brought it to her lips, kissing the tips of his long fingers slowly, one at a time. He stared at her and hunger erupted in his eyes, so intense she had to look away, focusing her concentration on bringing him pleasure. Her moves were no longer meant to soothe his aches; now they were about showing him, in perhaps the only way he'd understand, that she wanted *him* and no one else—that he was perfect for her and her alone.

Katie released his hand, reaching up to pull his face close enough so she could see the shadows forming where he'd shaved, and could smell that lemon-and-mint scent of his she'd always loved. She let her eyes wander over his gorgeous features: unruly hair, hazel eyes, sharp, high cheekbones, sexy stubble, full lips. She lingered there and then leaned in, kissing him delicately at first, exploring the soft flesh of his mouth with her tongue, then deeper until he reached for her, pulling her onto her knees and into his chest. She laid her palms against the hard surface, pushing him down onto his back, then lifted the hem of her dress and straddled him, taking control.

He slid his hands around her waist under the folds of her dress, plying her soft flesh with his fingers until she pulled the garment over her head, exposing a plum-colored satin-and-lace bra. She reached around her back and unhooked the clasp, pulled it over her shoulders, and let it slide down and off her arms.

Ryan's lips turned up at the corners and he

gave a soft, lazy laugh, the sound of it giving her all the confidence she needed to keep going.

Katie returned his laugh before silencing him with a finger over those lips of his, knowing there would be plenty of time to feel them all over her later.

She grasped at his button-down shirt and he raised his torso to slip it off for her, lifting up to pull his undershirt over his head before leaning back on his palms. His abs tensed with the effort of supporting his upper body, and she ran her hands over the firm muscles, stopping at the waistband of his trousers.

Looking into his eyes, she saw her hunger mirrored there, so she pulled the zipper down carefully over the hard bulge beneath the layers of denim and cotton. He lifted his backside and she eased the pants down and off his long legs, tossing them in a heap over the side of the bed.

He leaned back on his elbows and watched her as she undressed fully for him, openly admiring her pregnant form. Even the cool air of his hotel room didn't faze her, and she didn't move to hide her body. She wasn't afraid of being exposed—she felt strong and womanly, surprised at the sensation of enjoying the feel of her own skin. The delight she saw in his eyes as he stared at her figure didn't hurt, either, and she smiled as she returned his stare, surveying the long, muscular form at her feet.

The throbbing ache between her legs was growing too intense to handle much longer, but she would force herself to wait. She lowered herself back to the bed and crawled on her hands and knees until she hovered over him.

She opened her mouth and pressed her tongue against the flesh between his pecs, trailing it down, down, down to his belly button and farther south to the hem of his snug, black boxer briefs. Sitting back on her haunches between his legs, she wrapped her palms around the hard curve of his bottom, peeling the shorts off until he was gloriously naked. He reached to the floor beside the bed for his pants, grabbing a condom from his wallet.

"Katie," he said, his voice husky, the sound making her want him even more.

She pulled away and he groaned, both of them suffering the loss of skin on skin.

"Yes?" she said innocently, running her palms over the chiseled shape of his pelvic bones.

"Come here," he rasped, his voice thick under heavy breathing.

"Why should I do that?" she asked, continuing to tease his skin.

She guessed he'd finally had enough when he gripped both of her wrists and pulled her hips closer to his waist, then wrapped a hand over each of her full breasts.

The urgency of the movement delighted her. She was powerful, desired by this incredible man—a man who wanted her now in a way she'd always wished for.

She was the same Katie who'd grown up next door to Ryan—the same one who'd known from the instant they met that he was the one she wanted always. And even with her pregnancy, he made her feel confident, beautiful and sexy in her own skin. She didn't need to try to hide her feelings from him anymore.

"Because you're driving me crazy and I want you, Katie. Right now."

Katie obeyed, moving forward. She raised her hips slightly and then brought her body down, closing her eyes in ecstasy as he slid into her. His body filled every inch, every crevice of her, and she stayed there for a moment just savoring the bliss of having him this way, finally.

When need became too strong to ward off any longer, she let go—of everything—feeling Ryan alongside her the whole way, both of them trembling as she crashed, satisfied and full, into his arms.

A short while later, he grabbed her and took over, lighting her on fire over and over again, bringing them to satisfaction until they were both sated.

As daylight slipped through the hotel room curtains, Ryan woke slowly and happily, then studied the exhausted beauty sleeping on his chest, her head of raven hair rising and falling with each breath, a creamy arm strewn lazily across his abdomen.

He had so much work to do, so much to discuss with his father, and there were calls to make to check on business back in Seattle. Plus, he knew he should get Katie back home before her roommate started to worry, but he didn't want to wake her.

He reached out his free arm and wrapped the blanket tighter around Katie's shoulders, careful not to stir her.

God, she's gorgeous.

He'd imagined them together like they were last night many, many times, but none of those daydreams had lived up to what it was really like to make love to Katie Bloom.

She was perfect, every inch of her…perfect

for him. The memory of last night had him aroused again within minutes, but there would be time for that later…for as long as she would have him. He knew what it was like to live life without her, and he didn't want to do that anymore.

Chapter Twelve

Ryan pushed back the sheets and rose from the bed, tucking the snow-white down blanket around Katie's smooth shoulders, admiring her sleeping figure once again before heading for a shower.

Half an hour later, he'd dressed in jeans and a T-shirt and was puttering around the kitchenette, waiting for coffee to brew, when he heard the water come on in the bathroom. Just knowing Katie was in there made him smile, until he remembered.

Crap. There wasn't any decaf in the room for her. He knew it would probably be safe for her to have a single cup of real coffee, but in case she was being extra careful, he wanted to have the weaker stuff on hand when she came out of the room.

He considered ringing the concierge, but decided instead to just trek down to the desk himself; it would be much quicker and would save him the awkwardness of having someone bring it to his room before Katie was dressed. He planned to order her breakfast later, but didn't want to startle her before she'd had a chance to bathe and put something on.

The concierge procured the requested coffee within seconds, and Ryan headed back to the room, taking the stairs this time to get rid of some of the pent-up energy he was holding, probably a side effect of his new excitement over Katie.

He slipped his keycard into the door and opened it, expecting to hear or see her moving around the room, but he was met with complete, eerie silence, so thick that it made the fine hairs on his arms stand on end.

"Katie?" he called, hoping to hear her voice immediately.

Nothing.

"Katie?" he said, hearing the worry in his own tone. He dropped the pouch of decaf on the ground, his heart racing as he ran to the bathroom.

Oh, God.

"Katie." He was shouting now, his pulse thundering in his ears as he rushed toward her crumpled form, her dark hair sprawled out on the bathroom floor, her beautiful skin now sickeningly pale.

He lifted her head off the floor and held it in his lap, careful not to move her too much for fear he might harm her further.

He pulled out his phone to call 9-1-1 when Katie's head lifted slightly, and her eyes fluttered open.

"What happened?" she asked, and if he hadn't been so startled, Ryan would have reached down to kiss her; never in his life had he been so glad to hear her voice.

He set the phone aside, placing his palms on Katie's cheeks to steady her.

"Oh, Katie, I'm so glad you're awake."

"Ryan? What happened, Ryan? I was standing in the bathroom and then I felt a little woozy and the next thing I know…I'm on the floor."

"Do you know if you hit your head?" he asked, his eyes scanning every inch of her skin to check for marks.

She blinked a few times and Ryan worried he would lose her again. "Stay with me, baby, okay?" he pleaded. When she nodded, he repeated his question.

"I can't be sure, but I don't think so. I just sort of…knelt down, trying to lie flat so I wouldn't fall because I felt so weird. And then I guess…I guess I must have blacked out or something, because I don't remember anything after that."

"Just hang tight, okay? We've got to get you to the hospital."

As he began dialing, she opened her mouth and he half expected her to argue that she'd be fine, but then she touched her stomach, and Ryan knew she would give in to his demand that she get checked out, just to make sure the baby was okay.

The woman might be strong-willed, but Ryan knew her plenty well to know that she would never take a risk when it came to her kid.

He spoke to the operator and was informed that an ambulance was on its way, which he repeated to Katie.

While they waited, he drilled her for every piece of her medical history until she became exasperated with him.

"Ryan Ford!" she said, laughing, "I'm going to be fine. I've just been having some dizzy spells lately.

"Dammit, Katie, I knew it was a dumbass idea to let you go to that Pumpkin Fest in your condition."

"Oh, for Pete's sake, Ryan! Pregnant women

do all sorts of active things now. This isn't the 1950s. It was absolutely fine for me to go out there, and I don't think this has anything to do with the weekend."

She closed her eyes, realizing that what she'd just admitted would do the opposite of making him feel better.

"What the hell do you mean?"

"I mean…I've been having dizzy spells for a week or so. I didn't think anything of it before, but now I know I should have gotten it checked out before I left for that trip."

Ryan shook his head, beyond glad that she was okay enough to make him mad as hell, but…mad as hell.

"How could you have spent all that time with me and not said a word about how you were feeling?"

"I don't know," she said, sounding as if she meant it.

"Katie, I think you've been doing this alone for so long that you've gotten too stubborn to let anyone help you."

She bit her lip, looking adorable even then, with her hair all awry and her skin pale as snow. Ryan caught sight of a red welt blooming on her elbow, probably from when she'd hit the ground. Fresh anger filled him that he'd not been there when she needed him to be.

"I'm sorry, Ryan. I didn't mean to burden you like this."

Even more than seeing her body—lifeless, he'd thought, to be honest—unmoving on the ground only moments before, Katie's words cut Ryan to the bone.

"How could you say that, Katie? You could never be a burden to me. That's not what I meant. I just meant I…I want you to tell me these things from now on. I want you to let me take care of you."

A single tear formed in her eye and slid down the perfect skin of her cheek.

"I know that ex of yours might not have had the balls to stick around and be a dad, but I'm not him, Katie. If you want me to, if you'll let me, I'll be there for you."

Katie turned her head and tucked her face into Ryan's jeans, and he pulled her close until he could wrap his arms around her, fairly certain now that she didn't have any broken bones or injured places to which he could cause damage.

It seemed as if time slowed down and hours passed as Ryan stroked her hair, waiting for the ambulance to show up to carry his Katie to the hospital. He made a quick call down to the front desk to inform the concierge of what had happened and to let him know that EMTs would arrive shortly. When they finally knocked on the hotel room door, Ryan let them in, staying out of their way so they could give Katie their full attention. He stood helplessly by as they pulled out their equipment and set to work, checking her vital signs and getting her ready for transport.

One of the paramedics spoke to Ryan before they rolled Katie from the room in a fold-out wheelchair to let him know that, other than a rapid heartbeat, she seemed to be doing okay now, but they were glad he'd called because tests needed to be run to make sure she and the baby were well.

Ryan thanked him and stopped at the ambulance to say goodbye to Katie, pressing his lips against her forehead as she clasped his hand, her expression betraying the true extent of her worry.

"Everything's going to be fine," he said, squeezing her cold hand. "I'm following the ambulance to the hospital and I'll be right there with you."

Ryan waved as the uniformed medics carted her away, hoping she knew that he meant those words in every way possible.

The pace at the hospital was alarmingly brisk compared to the molasses speed with which time had moved back at Ryan's hotel room. It wasn't until a doctor had taken Katie back for an examination and tests, leaving him with nothing to do but wait, that he was able to sit down.

He hated the biting medical scent that filled the air now—that particular blend of sterilization, alcohol and illness that only hospitals could master. It was strange, he supposed, that he'd ended up in a profession that specialized in creating the type of buildings he found himself in...but then, he hadn't always despised them so much.

It was only when Sarah had ended up in one to give birth, only for both of them to walk away empty-handed, that Ryan had grown to loathe the smell of medical facilities.

Without anything to occupy him, he became hyperaware of his surroundings, noting several scattered attempts at cheer. There was a vase of tulips on the front desk, the flower petals unnervingly bright against the white backdrop, like a clown's garish face paint, and the muted colors of the generic pastels adorning the walls.

He made a note of what to request when he

and his father met with the interior designer they'd chosen to decorate the cancer treatment facility. Usually that part of the job was beyond his call of duty, but he saw now how much those seemingly small things mattered to people stuck in the waiting room, and he didn't see the point of making their hard days any gloomier. There was a lot that could be done to add a sense of calm to the room, and Ryan would put in his two cents if it would help make that difference.

He remembered Katie shoving her cell phone into his hand as the paramedics had wheeled her out of the room, and he grabbed it out of his pocket, navigating its interface until he found her list of contacts. Ryan pulled up listings for June, Katie's mother and father, and the elderly Mrs. Bloom and wrote a quick text to let them all know that he was with her, that she was safe and doing okay so far, and that he would keep them posted as he obtained updates.

Ryan should have known that her family wouldn't wait around, and it wasn't long until he received a worried phone call from Katie's mother, which he took as calmly as possible, letting her know that, no, she and Katie's dad did not need to fly in from their vacation in Vancouver and that, yes, the doctors had said she was probably fine and there was no need to worry.

Before she hung up, Katie's mom, never one to beat around the bush, also made sure to let Ryan know she was so glad he was back and that she hoped he'd stick around this time.

He hung up, shaking his head at the Bloom women, just in time to see Katie's grandmother rush through the door, June, still in her waitressing apron, at her side.

"Oh, my God, Ryan!" June said, rushing over, Mrs. Bloom hot on her heels. "Is Katie okay?"

"As far as I know, yes. But I'm still waiting for legitimate news."

"I'm so glad you were there for her," June said, patting his knee. He was thankful she didn't go into detail about Katie's whereabouts last night. She was a grown woman and could draw her own conclusions; plus, the two of them had been like peas in a pod since elementary school, and he was pretty sure Katie told June just about everything. Still, he was grateful she had the intuition to know he wasn't up for teasing, and she just sat there next to him, her presence comforting.

Katie's grandmother hugged his neck and

listened in as he'd spoken to June, so he didn't have to repeat himself, and then he asked after Shelby.

She gave him a quick update to let him know that things looked promising—she didn't have any real news to give him yet, but when she'd spoken to the director of the adoption agency, the woman had shown interest and didn't seem put off by the fact that he wasn't married and was a working man. He ached for the older children that were often overlooked in the system, but in this case, he hoped the lack of parental interest in her so far might work in his favor.

June talked with him a bit more, telling him goofy jokes from her bartender friend at work in an effort to cheer him up, but he could barely crack a smile.

It was hours later that Ryan saw the doctor

he'd met earlier coming down the hallway, a mask hanging around the neck of his blue scrub shirt.

The doctor gave Katie's little gathered posse a friendly smile, probably one he'd given hundreds of worried families over the years.

"Mr. Ford?" he said, reaching out to shake Ryan's hand. "We spoke earlier. I'm Dr. Green and I'll be taking care of Katie tonight."

"Tonight?" Mrs. Bloom asked.

"Yes," Dr. Green answered. "I'm afraid we'll need to keep Katie overnight to run a few more tests and to monitor her and the baby, just to make sure she's okay."

Ryan nodded, but his insides were screaming. Why would they need to keep her if she was truly doing all right, as the doctor had said? What were they keeping from him that he might need to know?

"I thought you said earlier that she was fine," Ryan stated, hearing the agitation in his own tone. He hadn't meant for it to be so clear that he was upset, but he couldn't seem to hide it in the face of possible danger to Katie.

The doctor folded his hands together. "We do believe she'll be fine, Mr. Ford, but we need to find out with absolute certainty." The youngish man looked from Ryan to Mrs. Bloom to June as he spoke, making sure to include all of them.

"It seems that Katie has early-onset pre-eclampsia, and we have to run some studies to determine if going without treatment has harmed the child."

Ryan had heard of preeclampsia before and knew the term indicated high blood pressure during pregnancy, but he didn't have any idea what the symptoms were or what kinds of effects it could cause. If he'd known, he would have watched her more closely, could have kept her from going to the Pumpkin Fest, even, if that would have kept her safe.

Was it possible she'd been in danger over the past few days, and he hadn't even known it? How could he be so careless with the woman he was rapidly falling for?

The doctor must have sensed Ryan's agitation because he stepped forward just a bit, holding up a palm. "This is quite common and, if well managed, can be nothing. Katie's about nineteen weeks along, and I've contacted her ob-gyn to head down as soon as she's available to check on Ms. Bloom. It seems Katie was previously unaware of her condition, and it's likely the symptoms only began recently."

"What are they? The symptoms, I mean?"

Ryan asked, shoving his hands into his jeans pockets to stop their wild fidgeting.

"Well, they can vary widely from patient to patient," the doctor answered, "but the most common signs are swelling in the legs and feet…sometimes even the hands…abdominal pain, headaches, vision changes, dizziness—"

Dizziness. Katie's woozy spells the past few days were part of this condition.

Ryan kicked himself for not forcing her to get to a doctor sooner.

Dr. Green continued, "It doesn't usually show up until the second half of pregnancy, usually in the later part of the second or early in the third trimester, but sometimes it can pop up earlier. It's a little strange to see it in someone as young as Katie, I must admit—it's more common in women over thirty, people with diabetes and mothers carrying more than one child, but it's not unheard-of by any means."

"Thank you, doctor," he said, his mind already elsewhere. "Keep us posted, will you?"

"Of course, sir," he answered as Ryan turned and headed down the hallway, leaving Mrs. Bloom and June behind. He would have to explain later. Right now, he had to get out of there immediately, had to get as far away from the hospital as possible so he could clear his head. As soon as the glass double doors came into view, Ryan broke into a run, escaping the dreadful hospital smell before he exploded.

Ryan didn't have any idea where he was going; he only knew he needed to run.

He drove back to the hotel room and, on autopilot, changed into training shoes, shorts and an old, thin T-shirt from a 5K years ago.

What was wrong with him?

Why couldn't he protect the person he cared about—the person he now knew he loved—more than anyone else in the entire world?

What was so terrible about him that he seemed to lose what he tried hardest to keep safe?

He'd married Sarah so that he could be there for her through a situation he was an equal party to; he'd helped her remember to take her vitamins and fed her healthy dinners, had lifted everything for her so she wouldn't have to, and still they'd lost their little girl.

Ryan ran the trail around his hotel without seeing the path in front of him. The only thing he could focus on without toppling over in pain was putting one foot in front of the other; he would keep moving forward until his head was clear, until he could think about how to tell Katie that he simply wasn't good enough for her.

He was the common factor in so much heartbreak—he'd known about his father's cheating and hadn't said a word, he'd been the cause of Sarah's disappointment in their marriage and…even though he knew it was illogical, he couldn't help but wonder if, somehow, he'd inadvertently lost them their baby.

He wasn't about to bring that kind of pain into Katie's life.

He would make sure she was cared for, would give her more money than she'd ever need, but maybe…maybe it was best if he kept his distance. Perhaps then she would have a chance at happiness, at a full life with her baby.

Ryan ran until sweat poured down his face and into his eyes, relishing the stinging punishment the saltwater caused. Surely he deserved it.

He stopped running and folded his body onto a bench, letting his face fall into his hands as he faced the hard truth that perhaps the best thing he could do for Katie was to simply stay the hell out of her life.

Chapter Thirteen

Katie blinked into the unfamiliar fluorescent light, waking to find herself in the white sea of a hospital room, the first part of her day a fuzzy mess.

She remembered collapsing, and waking in Ryan's arms, then riding to the hospital in an ambulance, but the rest was blurry and Katie was too tired to try to put the pieces together to make sense of them.

The only thing she cared about, the first thing that came to mind, was: *Where is my Ryan?*

She'd held on to the sound of his voice earlier on the bathroom floor, had latched on to it like the beams from a lighthouse in a wild storm, but now all she heard was a cacophony of strange whirs and beeps coming from the various machines she was attached to.

A nurse with beautiful chocolate-colored skin and huge hazelnut eyes stepped into Katie's room, smiling to find her patient awake.

"Well, hello, Ms. Bloom," the nurse said. "My name is Ashley." The nurse strode to the side of Katie's bed, checking the machine monitors and making notations on her clipboard. "How are you feeling, doll?" she asked.

Katie blinked a few more times and swallowed, her throat as dry as the grass during a Texas summer.

Ashley moved quickly to pour water from a pitcher, handing the glass to Katie, who drank greedily to satiate her fierce thirst.

Her throat a little moister now, Katie tried speaking. "What happened?" she asked.

Ashley stopped writing and met Katie's eyes. "You just had a little episode, is all," the nurse said. "I'll let the doctor give you more specific information once he settles on a diagnosis, but we think you're having some very minor preeclampsia."

Katie nodded, feeling a little nauseous all of a sudden.

"It doesn't seem to be too serious, and your vital signs are stable, but the doctor wants to keep you overnight, just to make sure you're good as new when you leave here."

Katie frowned and felt tears forming.

"Now, now, don't do that. You and your baby are going to be just fine."

"I feel so guilty," she said, and the nurse put her clipboard down on the bedside table.

"Why do you say that?"

Katie wiped at her eyes, feeling silly for crying in front of a stranger. She was pretty sure the sweet, attentive nurse saw all sorts of things in her daily work, but Katie didn't like the thought of being an emotional mess in the presence of someone she hardly knew.

"Well, I've been having these…dizzy spells…for a while now, and I noticed that my feet were a little puffier than usual, and I did nothing about it." She shook her head at her foolishness. "I could have kept this from happening. I should have talked to my doctor sooner. What kind of mother am I?"

Ashley glanced over at Katie's chart, then pulled a stool next to the bed. She sat, reaching out to hold the hand that rested on the side rail of Katie's bed. "Listen," she said, her soft voice drowning out Katie's need to punish herself for putting her child in danger. "I see that this is your first kiddo, yes?"

Katie nodded and the nurse went on.

"You are way, way too new to this game to start kicking yourself for making a tiny mistake. Let me tell you something that I've learned after a hundred years in this business."

Katie was skeptical. Ashley appeared no more than maybe ten years her patient's senior, but the woman seemed to know what she was talking about, so Katie listened. She figured after today, she could use just about any advice anyone might be willing to give her.

"No mother is perfect, and you will be no exception. You will make plenty of mistakes, and you will have days in which you want to run screaming from the most important job in the world, but if you love your kid, and you do the best you can at all times, everything will be just fine."

Katie squeezed her eyes shut and tears streamed down her face.

"Oh, honey, that's just the hormones," Ashley said, letting go and giving Katie's hand a pat. "You'll get used to them if you're not already."

She laughed and used a tissue the nurse handed her to wipe her eyes. When her mind cleared and she was able to think a little bit more coherently, she remembered that she hadn't seen Ryan.

Katie asked Ashley if she could find him

for her, and the kind nurse checked her vitals again before grabbing her clipboard and leaving the room, promising to send in Dr. Green and her regular ob-gyn as soon as possible. But Katie didn't want to see either of them.

She only wanted Ryan Ford.

He'd been so attentive, so sweet back at his hotel room, taking such good care of her. Surely he hadn't behaved that way just because they'd slept together?

That seemed unlikely, given the way he'd spoken to her last night, the way he'd told her he wanted to be a part of her and her baby's lives. He'd said he wanted to take care of her and spend far more time with her.

So where the hell is he now?

Katie picked up her glass to take another sip of water, letting the cool liquid slide down her still-dry throat.

If she could've found her phone, she would have texted him, but she searched the small table by her hospital bed and it wasn't there. Finally, exhausted, she curled into a ball and attempted to sleep, trying hard not to think about the fact that he was nowhere to be found at the very second she needed him the most.

Ryan's phone, always a little busy, was buzzing with such frequency he briefly wondered if the apocalypse had come while he'd been running, and escaped his notice.

He pulled it out of his jeans pocket and stared at it, full of guilt.

The most recent text was from June, who was back at the hospital with Katie—the hospital he really should have stayed at—and, from the number of times an expletive popped up in her short narratives, was mad as hell.

It had not been his intention to worry anyone, and it certainly was not because he was attempting to run from his problems. Ryan knew as well as anyone that such a thing wasn't possible.

No. It was something different; a sort of panic had set off inside of him like an alarm, warning him that if he didn't get out of there soon, he might explode.

So, he'd busted through the front doors of the hospital and started running, first to his car and then, when he'd dressed for it, all the way around Peach Leaf.

Now he rubbed his eyes as he pulled up to the familiar old house, looking forward to the visit ahead about as much as one would a root canal.

But he knew what he needed to do.

He didn't deserve to let Katie love him until

he was exactly the kind of man she needed and the kind he wanted to be. Honest, true and capable of forgiveness.

He shoved his foot on the parking brake with more force than necessary, letting some of his body's pent-up energy go. This would not be easy. Hell, he wasn't even sure it was possible, but he would do it for Katie; he would do anything for Katie.

He knew now, without even the slightest shadow of doubt, that he loved her and that he wanted to spend the rest of his life with her. All of it—from the very highest moment of happiness to, God forbid, the lowest low.

But he had to do this first.

Ryan opened the door and stepped out of his truck, pausing to lean against the vehicle and study the house he grew up in.

Aside from his father's affair and the resulting damage, Ryan had many good memories from his childhood. His mother had made the perfect home; it was beautiful like the rooms from a home and garden magazine and had mostly been full of warmth. She did all the things she could to make his life comfortable and safe. Even though she spent a great deal of her time volunteering and giving her time to others with greater need than their family, she still somehow managed to give Ryan all the attention he needed.

When he'd come home from school, the house was always filled with the scent of baking cookies, and she would join him with a glass of milk to ask about his day, listening intently to his every word as though they were the most important things in her world. Then his mother, the sharply intelligent Harvard grad, would help him with his homework, making sure he realized the importance of reading, of education, before letting him run off to play with his friends. He'd enjoyed a lot of good times before his father's affair, before the clipped, quiet arguments he heard at night behind his parents' bedroom door when they thought he'd been asleep. His mother had tried so hard to shield him from the more painful sides of life, and he supposed he respected that—he imagined that when the time came, he would do the same, but it hadn't helped him in the end. His world had been so sheltered as a beloved only child that he'd ended up lacking the coping skills it required to be a good man.

His hasty departure from the hospital was the perfect example.

He knew in his heart that he should have stayed, and he knew he would have to go back and face the consequences of his actions after he was done here; he just hoped Katie would be able to see the real him and let him back in once more.

He stared up at the large white Victorian, its wraparound porch surrounded by pristine landscaping…and then he dared a look next door.

Katie's house.

Butter yellow, with a porch covered in an array of pots filled with bougainvillea, her home wasn't anywhere near as large or immaculate as Ryan's parents', but he knew it contained far more warmth.

All right, enough.

It was time.

Ryan stepped up to the porch and placed a hand on the polished brass knocker, pounding it into the door three times.

He didn't realize he'd been holding his breath until it opened and his eyes landed on his mother.

"Mom," he said, lurching forward to wrap her in his arms before she even had a chance to speak. Her frame felt only slightly thinner than it had in the past, he noticed as he held her. He was glad there was still meat on her bones in the wake of her illness and, even though her snowy hair wasn't as thick as it had always been, the change was so subtle that Ryan couldn't be sure if it was a result of the cancer or her age; he hoped for the latter.

"Oh, Ryan, honey," she said, squeezing her arms around him before backing away to get a better look. "I'm so glad you're here."

She stepped back from the doorway and waved an arm. "Come on in, son."

Ryan obeyed, following her down the shining marble floor of the foyer. He wasn't surprised when she led him to the kitchen, and he half expected her to pull a sheet of cookies out of the oven, but instead, she pulled out two mugs and filled a kettle with water.

"That's okay, Mom," he said, smiling when she turned from fussing with a blue enamel tea caddy. "You don't have to make me anything."

"Nonsense," she said, turning back to choose two bags. "You look like you could use a cup of tea. Besides, it'll ensure that you stick around for more than five minutes."

"How are you feeling?" he asked, his voice betraying his worry. "Are you getting enough rest?"

"Hush now, Ryan. I don't want to talk about that. I want you to tell me how you're doing. How is that successful firm of yours?" Her eyes, still the vivid blue they'd always been, shined, and he could see how happy she was to have him sitting in her kitchen. For a second, he couldn't recall why it was he'd stayed away for so long.

Suddenly, seeing his mother join him at the kitchen table was far more important than any of the reasons he'd dreamed up over the years for staying away. Yes, they had their vacations together, but somehow it wasn't the same. His mother had always been a woman who loved her home, and she looked at peace there in a way she never had on their trips.

Ryan did what she asked and caught her up on his business, which they hadn't discussed the week before. She was pleased to hear that it was still doing well, saying as much before she peppered him with more questions. After she'd poured their tea, they talked for over an hour, and it felt good to laugh with her again.

Suddenly, his mom's mood changed and she looked down into her tea. Ryan reached out for her hand, afraid she was going to tell him that her cancer was worse, but instead, she asked him about Katie.

"Your father mentioned you took her to the Pumpkin Fest," his mom said, her eyes crinkling at the corners. "I was very glad to hear that, you know."

Ryan swallowed over the boulder that appeared in his throat at the mention of Katie's name. "Yes, I did."

"And?" his mom asked, clasping a warm hand over his cool one.

"And," he answered, unable to keep a smile from his voice, "She's…Katie. Still the same old wonderful, gorgeous Katie."

His mom's eyes darkened a shade. "But…"

Ryan inhaled slowly and let the air back out. "But…I messed up with her again." He met his mother's eyes. "I seem to have a particular knack for screwing up when it comes to that girl."

"Well, son, to tell the truth, I wasn't happy when you married Sarah." She held up a hand to keep him from speaking before she'd finished what she had to say. "I know you had your reasons, but I always thought you and Katie would…end up together." She took a sip of her tea and pulled away the hand that held his, wrapping both of hers around her mug. "She's always been the perfect woman for you, Ryan."

"I know that, Mom. I know. I think it just… took a long time for me to see that, even though it seems so obvious. I think part of me was just afraid."

His mother narrowed her eyes and her eyebrows knit together. "Afraid of what, son?"

Ryan drained the last of his tea and set his mug down on the table's old, finished oak surface. "Afraid of losing her, I guess, even though I never really had her to begin with, did I?" He gave a sad chuckle. "And mostly, I was—am—afraid I'm not a good enough man for her."

His mom's eyes filled with moisture and Ryan had to look away to keep his from doing the same.

"Ryan," she said, "what happened with your and Sarah's baby wasn't your fault. You had nothing to do with the death of that child."

He studied his hands as she spoke to keep a bundle of raw emotions from taking over.

"You have to let her go if you're going to give your heart to someone else."

"That's just the thing, though. You see, Katie's pregnant and the father, well, he's a total ass, but the thing is, I want to be there for her, if she'll have me. I want to be a dad to her baby, but I'm not sure I can go through that again. She's at the hospital now. She collapsed and I took her there. The doctor says it's preeclampsia and that she'll be okay, but I just don't know if I can handle losing another child…or losing her."

Annabelle Ford closed her eyes and then opened them again before shoving her mug aside. "Listen, son," she said. "You have got to stop thinking like that. You have to stop being afraid of something that happened when you were barely more than a child, and get on with your life. I'm sorry to have to put it so frankly, but there it is, Ryan."

He nodded, knowing she was right, even though it was hard to admit, hard to let her words sink into the place in his heart that needed them to heal.

"Life is full of hard things, son. You can't let that stop you from living it." She smiled. "You're only here for such a short time, anyway. Even if you insist on being a stubborn ass, you might as well make the best of it."

Ryan felt a laugh begin deep in his belly, and as his mother's wisdom began to filter in, a ray of hope shot through him, and he knew that he could do this. He could finally let go of the baby he'd lost and, if Katie would let him, he'd be the best father he could for the little one he hoped she'd share with him.

There was just one more thing he had to do first.

Chapter Fourteen

After promising his mom he would return later for dinner, Ryan left the kitchen and headed down the hallway, stopping in at a powder room to splash his face.

After years of believing he hated his father, he was surprised to find that, after seeing Katie in potential danger and after speaking with his mother, all he had left in him was low-grade agitation and disappointment.

He wasn't sure if he would ever be able to

completely get over what had happened. From where he stood, he was sure his distaste for what his dad had done to his mom would always remain somewhere in the background; it might become easier to tolerate, like the hum of a hearing aid or a consistent, dull pain, but the truth was, no matter how hard he tried, he would never be able to look at his father again and see the man he'd known *before*.

Forgive and forget, the adage preached.

The forgiveness, Ryan thought, he could manage, or at least he could work on it and hope to get better with time, but did anyone ever truly forget the deep wounds of childhood?

But he owed it to Katie and her child to put his past behind him as best he could. And, if he was going to be a dad himself, he needed to be able to teach his kids that family was family and that unconditional love was paramount. Maybe, he thought, over time he would come to believe those things, though he would rather cut off his own arm than ever consider cheating on Katie.

To Ryan, love in its purest form should be a precious combination of loyalty, faithfulness, kindness and unfaltering support. He'd always expected it of others, and he wouldn't think of giving Katie any less than that.

He'd always held himself to high standards, and much of his disappointment in life was the result of being let down when the people in his world did not fulfill them.

He supposed he'd have to work on loosening up a little, on meeting the people in his life where they stood, rather than expecting absolute perfection from them.

After all, he wasn't perfect, so how could he expect everyone else to be?

Ryan paused at the last door on the right, raising his fist and then lowering it again, over and over, until he finally just bit the bullet and knocked.

"Come in," his father's gruff voice came from behind the door, and Ryan twisted the pewter knob to open it.

"Dad?" he said, facing his father, who was seated at his large cedar desk. The old man wore reading glasses and a stack of papers was sprawled in front of him.

"Hello, son," his father said, glancing up at Ryan before turning his attention back to the work. "Come on in and have a seat."

"Actually, if it's all the same to you, Dad, I'd prefer to stand."

Ryan's father put his pen down and met

his son's eyes. His were clouded with something that Ryan couldn't identify—confusion, maybe, or curiosity.

"That's just fine, son," he said, leaning back in his chair, setting his hands in his lap.

Ryan shoved his own hands into his pockets and began to pace, an old habit he returned to each time he had something important to get off his chest, or something stressful to get through, like a presentation at work. Speaking to his own father shouldn't have felt so difficult, but maybe Ryan could finally get out all the things he'd always needed to say to the older man. Then, perhaps, some of the tension would dissipate, or at least whittle down to something they could work through… together. Ryan was willing to do so if his father was.

He wandered the expansive office, studying

the bookshelves, noting the familiar leather volumes, the gilt-framed photographs of Ryan and his mother, of the three of them with family dogs over the years. He came to a particular one of his mother—one he'd never seen before. In the shot, Mom was sitting on a bench, a sketch pad or a notebook on her lap, Ryan couldn't be sure which, and she was looking off into the distance at something only she could see. Her eyes were the color of periwinkles, calm but full of life, like the river he and Katie swam in only a couple of days before. It was an incredibly simple, amateurish shot, but even a stranger could see that the photographer was completely enamored of its subject, of the wildly beautiful woman sitting there, heart full of dreams.

Ryan's stomach clenched.

"How could you do it, Dad?" he asked, the

mild tension in the room growing thicker in an instant. “How could you cheat on Mom?”

The question was direct, but Ryan’s voice wasn’t accusatory, merely sad and lost, which was exactly how he’d felt all those years ago upon finding out what his dad was up to behind his mother’s back.

Ryan didn’t turn to look at his father; he didn’t need to see what emotions were warring on the man’s face to know that he’d stirred something deep.

A long moment passed before his father cleared his throat, which did little to remove the gravel, or the genuine sorrow, from his voice.

“I want you to know that what I’m about to say is not my way of excusing what I did,” he said, pausing as if to measure his words carefully. "I know that what I did was unforgiveable, son, and it's not an excuse."

Ryan turned to face his father and what he saw jostled something in the very bottom of his heart. The older man's eyes were brimming with unshed tears, the normally hard ice-blue softened into cool water.

"Rather," he continued, "it's a reason."

Ryan stopped pacing and pulled out one of the leather chairs in front of the desk, sitting down. He folded his hands in his lap and loosened his clenched jaw, hoping his features were gentle enough to encourage his dad to go on.

"You see, son, your mom and I…we married very young. Younger even than when you married Sarah, and not for the same reason."

Ryan watched as his dad traveled through

his memories, settling on the day he'd first met Annabelle.

"I loved her dearly from the second I laid eyes on her, as cliché as that might sound. And, Lord knows why, she felt the same. We wed right when I graduated, when she was still a junior in high school. That wasn't so strange back then."

He hesitated, seeming to think about the past before he could move on.

"I thought she'd hung the moon, your mom. She was such a beauty…still is," he said, grinning. "And we were happy for a long time, we really were." He frowned. "But things weren't perfect. We had our problems just like any other married couple and, after you were born, Annabelle became distant for a while. It may have been postpartum depression, or something else, I don't really know, and she always said she didn't need to talk to a physician about it. But that doesn't matter. What I'm trying to say is that we grew apart, and that division lasted for quite some time."

The older man's brows knit. "There was a period there when she said she wasn't sure she loved me anymore."

He closed his eyes and Ryan swallowed, concerned that if he moved too much, his father might lose the story that they both needed him to finish telling.

"When she said that, I just lost it. I was terrified of losing her, and that was a very real possibility at that point. She wasn't sure she wanted to stay married to me, and knowing that she might leave set something off in me. I don't know if I did what I did to get Annabelle's attention or to hurt her...I'm not sure, but I don't think so. It's hard to see clearly when you're looking at the past."

Ryan sat perfectly still, listening…perhaps even starting to understand a little bit what his dad might have gone through. As the man had said, it didn't excuse anything, but it sort of…made things make more sense.

"I can't pinpoint why it happened…why I caused it to happen…but believe me when I say that if I could undo it, I would. A thousand times, I would."

Ryan was at a loss for words, and when he did speak, it was only to state something they both already knew. "You shouldn't have, Dad. And it wasn't okay to drag me into it."

"I know that, son. And I want you to know that I am so sorry."

His father choked up, rendering speech impossible for a moment.

"I love her more than anything in the world, and once she decided that she wanted me to stay, that she loved me, too, it was like a light turned on in my heart, and I'd realized what I'd done. I've spent every second of every day since trying to show her that I wish it had never happened and that I'm sorry."

Ryan nodded, trying to sort through his emotions, to make sense of the whirlwind.

"I should have said the same to you a long time ago, son. I'm so sorry."

Ryan swallowed, letting his father's words wash over a wound inside his heart. It was the first step, he hoped, to its healing.

"I accept your apology," he said. "And I'd like to…I'd like to work on repairing what we both broke here."

His father nodded and Ryan saw tears fall from the older man's eyes, for the first time in memory. And even though it took great strength to do so, even though it wasn't the most comfortable thing in the world and felt about as natural as poking himself with a needle, Ryan got up from his chair and headed around behind the desk. He stood with open arms, and his father rose to meet him, hugging his son tight.

They finally let go when they heard a knock on the office door and saw Annabelle standing there. It was odd, Ryan thought, to see her now, knowing another part of her past, but he was relieved to find that it didn't change anything about how much he loved his mom. She was the same person she'd always been, but with a few imperfections Ryan had never known about. Instead of tainting her in his eyes, the knowledge only seemed to make her character stronger to him. She'd suffered through some difficult things in her young marriage and had been the receiver of a few pretty hard blows in her life, not the least of which was the cancer she was battling as they stood there, but there she was, strong as the oak tree that shaded the front porch of his family home.

That was what he needed to be for Katie—sturdy and steady in even the most threatening storms that might come their way. He could bend and falter, but the important thing was for him to remain steadfast. He would learn from his parents' mistakes, rather than repeating them.

It was a relief to know, finally, that he didn't have to be perfect...he just had to be his very best for the woman he loved, and the children he wanted to have with her. He would be her strength when she lacked it and, hopefully, she would be the same for him. He didn't have to do this alone.

He loved Katie, and if he was lucky, maybe she loved him, too.

Chapter Fifteen

"Ease up, June, I'm not an invalid."

Katie appreciated her friend's concern, but she really wasn't interested in continuing to be treated as though she might keel over at any second. To be fair, that was what had gotten her into the hospital in the first place, but she knew what she needed to do now to keep it from happening again.

"That may be true, but your opinion on the subject is invalid."

"Oh, my God, June, I'm *so* not in the mood for stupid puns right now."

June just whacked her gently on the shoulder and kept pushing Katie's wheelchair until they reached the nurses' station.

"All right, Ms. Bloom," Ashley said when she'd completed the necessary paperwork to get her the heck out of there, "you're all set."

"Thanks so much for everything, Ashley. You were an absolute dream."

The nurse who'd taken care of Katie overnight waved her hand dismissively. "You weren't so bad yourself," she said, teasing. "Just do me a favor and make sure you don't end up back in here. Follow the doctor's discharge instructions and remember to take it easy. I don't want to see you again, you hear?"

Katie rolled her eyes, but the nurse wasn't having it. "What did I say?"

"All right, all right. I'm supposed to take it easy, I know."

June pinched Katie hard on the shoulder.

"Ow! What was that for?"

"For sassing the nurse. You heard what she said, and I am not going to let you alone again until this baby is born and you're both healthy."

"Really," Katie asked, overdramatizing her rubbing of the sore spot to make June feel as badly about it as possible. "And how do you plan to do that with a full-time job?"

June stopped pushing the wheelchair and sat in one of the waiting room chairs just inside the sliding glass doors. Turning Katie's chair to face her, she bit her lip and Katie could tell her friend was up to no good.

"What is it, June?" she demanded. "What are you not telling me?"

June didn't say anything, but Katie caught her eyes focusing on something across the room.

She turned to find Ryan standing a few yards away, an incredible bouquet of soft pink roses and baby's breath in his hands; the arrangement was so large it covered up most of his torso.

Her breath caught as she met his eyes and he began walking toward her. Her emotions were such a confusing mess that she couldn't figure out whether to scream at him for leaving her again or to grab him and hold on for dear life in the hope that it would not happen again…much the way she'd reacted when she'd first seen him back in Peach Leaf only a few days before.

"Ryan," she said, her voice sounding defeated even to her own ears.

He didn't say anything, just stood there looking apologetic and handsome and…in love.

Finally, he leaned forward to give her the flowers, bracing himself on her wheelchair as he lowered himself to his knees.

She looked over her shoulder at June, who was staring at the couple as though they were in a movie. Katie pulled a face at her friend, who just waved her away, grabbing a tissue to wipe her eyes.

"First of all, I'm not proposing, so you can stop freaking out right about now—" Katie couldn't help but grin through her frustration "—and second, there are about a thousand things I need to tell you…that I've needed to tell you for far too long."

She looked down at the discharge papers in her lap, gathering her concentration. The moment was intense, full of sentiment, but though she wanted to let him speak, she needed to make sure that she had her bearings, that she could listen to his words with distance and wisdom, and not let her heart get in the way and cause her to make impulsive decisions.

She had a baby to think of…a baby that reminded her recently that he or she came first and that she needed to concentrate on taking care of the two of them before anyone else came into the picture. She'd known that before, but the past few days moved the knowledge to the very forefront, so that she had no choice but to face it head-on.

"Ryan, I'm sure you've got your reasons, and I know you're a good man, but I really don't think now's the time to—"

He reached up and gripped her hands tight, wrapping his around them until they covered hers completely, and he didn't show any signs of letting go.

"Look, Katie, just…let's not talk here. You must be starving, and this place makes me nervous and I'd really like to take you somewhere else so we can talk."

She gave him a look that probably expressed what she felt after spending the night in the hospital, doctors monitoring her every move, and June and her parents fussing over her as though she were a helpless child.

"You don't have to do anything, and you don't have to agree with me. The only thing I need you to do is let me give you something to eat and…listen to me."

His eyes were the kicker. She'd seen that look before and knew exactly what it meant: sheer determination.

Ryan Ford was not going to give up until she gave in.

She tilted her head. "I'll go with you, Ryan, on one condition."

"Anything," he said, his eyes pleading with her.

"I'm so sick of hospital food and I am starving, so for all that is holy, let me pick the place."

He smiled, looking immensely relieved. Even though there were things she needed to say to him, and things she needed to hear him say, and even though he'd better have a damn good reason to have hightailed it out of the hospital at a terrible time, she knew there was only one thing that truly mattered.

She loved him, and it was plain on his face that he loved her.

The rest they could handle together.

* * *

Katie had loved the fancy Italian place Ryan took her to the day before, but with the chaos over and the medical stuff behind her, hopefully until her next regular maternity checkup, she was in the mood for good old-fashioned comfort food.

She could smell the grease from the parking lot when they pulled into Barb's diner, and she inhaled deeply, letting the scent of Southern-fried food do its thing.

"I offer to take you anywhere in town and this is where you pick," Ryan said, shaking his head in wonder at the woman beside him in the truck. "You're something else, Katie Bloom."

It took a lot of convincing for Ryan not to carry her inside, and Katie wondered if he was trying to make up for leaving yesterday. The thought made her a little queasy and she unbuckled her seat belt, but didn't make a move to get out of the truck.

"Ryan," she said. "Before we eat, before you say anything or…just before anything else happens, I really need to know one thing."

He turned off the vehicle and removed his own safety belt, turning to face her, the motion the only signal she needed to continue.

"After all that happened over the weekend… going out there together, skinny-dipping in the river and…well, you know."

Neither of them needed a reminder of what else had happened.

If she closed her eyes, Katie could still feel Ryan's warm hands on her skin; she had spent a great deal of her time in the hospital reimagining the entire night.

She took a deep breath and found the courage she needed to go on.

"I need to know why you always run when things get tough," she said, her words setting off something that flickered across his features.

"I know you're a good man, Ryan, but I have to be honest with you. I'm not sure I can be with you if you can't stick around. I lost my heart when you left me for Sarah, and I thought I'd lost it again when you left me at the hospital. I can handle Bradley leaving, but I don't think I can handle it if you ever do that to me again."

She looked up, catching the sorrow in his green-gold eyes.

"I didn't love Bradley," she said, "but I do love you."

Ryan reached across the seat to grab her hand but she pulled away and pressed on.

"Say something, Ryan. Tell me why you did that. Tell me you won't do it again."

"Katie," he said, reaching again to touch her. This time she let him, encouraged by the fact that he'd tried again, even though it might have hurt him.

"The truth is, I left because I was afraid, too."

"Afraid of what?"

"Of losing you, Katie. You're all that matters to me in this world, and when you collapsed the other day, I couldn't face the fact that you might not get up again, that something truly bad might happen to you."

She nodded, hearing his words but not yet fully understanding.

"The baby that Sarah and I had?"

Katie nodded again.

"We lost it…we lost her," he said. "She wasn't alive when she was born. That was part of why Sarah and I couldn't stay together—there was just too much pain between us after that—but the other reason is that we never really loved each other."

Katie could no longer see past the tears that flooded her eyes, the pain of Ryan's words sinking in; she felt his loss almost as though it was her own, and she reached down to touch her belly, just to make sure she could still feel the form of the tiny being inside her.

It was her turn to reach for him then, and she scooted over on the seat, pulling him in close as he embraced her.

His apology was all there in the way he held her, stroking her long hair, but there was more he needed to say, and she was more than glad to hear it.

"I love you, Katie. I always have and I always will. When I ran away from the hospital yesterday, it was to take care of some things, so that when I came back, I could give you everything I have. I had to let my dad know that even though I'm not sure I can forgive him just yet, we're okay…or that we will be."

Ryan slid a finger down Katie's cheek, brushing away her tears before tucking it under her chin to tilt her face toward his.

"I don't want to be like my father. I don't want to make those kinds of mistakes. I want to be a man you can trust no matter what happens. I want you to know that I will never, ever leave you again, come hell or high water. I will take care of you and your…our…baby because I love you more than anything in the world, and I want you to be mine, Katie."

Her heart was so full that all she could manage in the way of communicating her answer was a happy nod.

In the space of only a few minutes, Ryan said all she ever wanted to hear, and it was more than enough to last a lifetime.

Epilogue

Katie giggled, unable to see on account of a bandanna blindfold, as they bumped along in Ryan's truck.

"Where are we going, crazy man?" she asked.

The only response was a whole lot of nothing.

But Ryan remained tight-lipped, refusing to say a word on the subject or even to give the tiniest of hints.

She reached behind her to the bundle strapped in a car seat in the back of the truck, tickling baby Michele's tiny feet.

One of these days, I'll get a first laugh out of that one, she thought.

Even though she wasn't biologically his, and though she was a sweet, happy baby, Katie's little girl had Ryan's serious intelligence.

She would catch the baby sometimes studying blocks or the toys hanging from her mobile as if she could already understand the way they functioned. She even hoped that Michele might someday go into the family business and take over her daddy's architecture firm.

All in good time, though, she chided herself. *Let the kid grow up first.*

Finally, the truck pulled to a stop.

"Are we there yet, Mom? I don't see anything." Shelby asked from the backseat, her voice groggy from sleep. Katie was glad at least one of them had gotten some rest on the long drive.

Ryan had pulled the three girls out of bed that morning, fed them stacks of peach pancakes and then hurried them along as they dressed and filed obediently into the car, none of them the wiser about where on Earth he was taking them.

He was so excited that Katie couldn't help but feel that way, too, knowing that if her husband had planned a surprise, it would be a good one.

"I don't know," Katie answered. "You'll have to ask your dad. He's the one in charge here." She giggled and Shelby directed her question toward Ryan, who still said nothing about their destination.

"All right, ladies. Out of the truck," he ordered, moving quickly to get himself out so he could help Shelby and the baby.

Katie, unfortunately, was still stuck with the blindfold.

Presumably holding the carrier in one hand, Ryan came round to her side of the truck and opened the door, grabbing her hand to help her down.

"This would be a heck of a lot easier if I could see, you know," she teased, but Ryan just laughed.

"Oh, I know. But where's the fun in that? This is a surprise, so, naturally, I want you to be surprised."

She rolled her eyes, slightly disappointed that no one could see her expression.

"Watch your step," he said before laughing. "Oh, right, I forgot."

Ryan told Shelby to stay close and not to

say anything as she followed behind. He led them down a gravelly road—Katie could feel the pebbles beneath her shoes and saw their white dust from the narrow open slit at the bottom of her bandanna.

After a few minutes, she heard Ryan set down the baby carrier, and he placed a hand softly on her elbow, leaning in to whisper in her ear.

"We're here, my love," he said, reaching around her head to untie the cloth. "Open your eyes."

She did, blinking at the vivid sun until her eyes adjusted to the light.

The first thing she saw was a long, red building in the distance.

"Horsies!" Shelby cried out, just as the word sprung into Katie's mind.

Then, scanning the view around her, she saw

several small buildings that looked like cabins, painted alternating bright, primary colors. There were names of various native Texan birds on little wooden plaques just outside the doors.

And then she saw water, which she'd thought she vaguely heard earlier, but had been too invested in walking without sight to think much about.

A river, wide and clear, flowing through what was obviously a camp, stretched far into the distance. After that, she noticed a swimming pool, tennis and basketball courts, and a long, low building that must have been a dining hall.

Tears welled up and Katie put her hands over her mouth.

"Ryan, is this—"

She looked up and the smile that spread

across his handsome face brought one to hers. He didn't even have to answer her.

"Do you like it?" he asked. "It's my family's land. It would have come to me eventually when my parents pass, but my father said there wasn't any reason for it not to be used now and, well, it's perfect for a new campsite, don't you think?"

She could barely speak, her mouth open wide in awe.

"This expansion is much larger than the museum's old campground, so it requires a full staff."

Katie nodded, normal human speech still eluding her. "That means that—"

Ryan smiled. "Yes," he said. "Everyone from the museum will have a job here if they want one. We've already hired on several of your coworkers, and we're expecting a few more to sign on soon. Plus," he said, pride filling his features, "we've got a full-time nurse now, in case anybody decides to get ahead of themselves and go to a Pumpkin Fest when they should be staying home, resting."

She gave his arm a little jab, and he grasped her hand, pulling her in close.

"All employees have full benefits packages and we've doubled their salaries."

Katie pushed her face into his shirt, so overwhelmed by joy that she couldn't do much else.

He tucked a finger under her chin, urging her to look into his eyes. "I did this for you, Katie," he said. "I know you hate that the museum is gone, but I'm hoping this will make you feel a little better."

She pulled back a little, so she could get the full view around her.

The campsite was amazing. Blue skies stretched out for miles and there were places for kids to do just about anything fun they could imagine. Horseback riding, swimming, roasting marshmallows over a campfire…it was all there.

Ryan was right. A little part of her would always miss the museum and her old job, but, when she was ready to go back to work, it looked as if there would be plenty to do at the new place for years to come. "Do you like it?" Ryan asked.

"Oh, my gosh, Ryan, it's perfect. It's the most amazing thing anyone's ever done for me!"

His eyes lit up at her compliment and he moved his face toward hers, pulling her close for a long kiss.

"Mom!" Shelby's shout snapped them apart.

“What, sweetheart?”

“There are horses! So many horses! Black ones and white ones and brown ones…”

Katie laughed and let her daughter lead her away as Ryan picked up Michele’s carriage to follow.

“Go on ahead,” he called out. “I’ll catch up, don’t worry.”

Shelby dragged Katie to the stables by her hand, not slowing down until they ran into Alvin, who looked particularly well and pleased to have such a fine new facility for the animals he loved so much.

After Shelby had met her new equine friends, Ryan took them all over to the dining hall, where the new chef made hamburgers for their family. They went horseback riding and Ryan played a game of basketball with

Shelby, while Katie and Michele looked on from the sidelines.

When night fell, they toasted marshmallows over a campfire, making s'mores out of graham crackers and chocolate that the chef provided. Katie delighted in Shelby's sticky mess and even Michele let out a high-pitched squeal at seeing her big sister's face covered in chocolate as though she'd grown a beard.

Ryan had brought everything the family needed to spend the night there, and after they'd tucked in Shelby, Katie carried a sleeping Michele out onto the front porch of the cabin they'd chosen and sat next to Ryan in a porch swing.

He patted her thigh and snuggled in close, and Katie remembered the night they'd gone swimming, stark naked in the river at the old campground. She laughed out loud.

"Penny for your thoughts?" Ryan asked.

"I was just thinking about that night we went skinny-dipping." She gave him a saucy look across the bundle in her arms. "I can't imagine what I was thinking, almost twenty weeks pregnant with this one. I had no business doing a striptease…outside! I was so nervous!"

Ryan laughed. "Nervous? I never would have guessed, not in a million years. You looked like you knew exactly what you were doing, and—" he leaned in close to whisper in Katie's ear "—you did a damn fine job."

Katie pressed her lips together in a straight line to keep from giggling and waking the baby. "Yes, nervous! I didn't exactly make a habit of shucking my clothes and jumping into rivers with half-naked men, you know."

Ryan wordlessly took Michele from Katie's

arms, placing a finger over his lips as he gently rocked her before walking back into the cabin.

Katie leaned back in the porch swing and looked up into the night sky. It was a deep, deep blue, almost black, and there were so many stars that they lit up their background almost as well as the sun. The moon was full and pale yellow, and Katie sent up a thank-you to the universe.

Everything she'd ever wanted was in the cabin behind her.

Ryan, Shelby, Michele…a family.

It was almost unbelievable how quickly her life had changed from daunting and filled with uncertainty to what could only be called perfection.

She rested her head against the wooden

swing, kicking her toes against the ground to push it back and forth.

Ryan returned a few moments later, his arms empty.

He clasped her fingers with his own and she smiled at the gleam of their new wedding bands as he pulled her from the seat by both hands, leading her away from the building and down to the water.

Katie hesitated and Ryan paused. "I know what you're thinking," he said. "But we're still close enough to see the cabin just fine, and I brought this." He smiled and pulled their baby monitor's parent unit from his pocket before squeezing her hand and continuing to walk.

Once they got to the shore, he removed her shirt and shorts slowly, his fingers gliding over her skin, waking up every inch of her body.

"I know you said you don't make a habit of swimming with naked men," he said, his cheek pressed against hers, lips close to her ear. "But I'd really like it if you would consider doing just that."

Katie reached down to grasp the bottom of his shirt, pulling it over his head in a single motion. "I'll think about it," she said, teasing as she unbuttoned his jeans.

When they were both undressed, Ryan counted to three and they jumped into the water, gasping and laughing as they recovered from having the wind knocked from their lungs.

As they swam under the starlight, their kids tucked safe inside, Katie knew that, no matter what came, no matter what challenges surfaced for her, Ryan or their children, they had everything they needed to make it through anything.

They were a family.

* * * * *